Lock Down Publications and Ca$h
Presents

I0664146

Killaz On Standby 2

By Any Means Necessary

Written By

IRA B.

First Edition 2025

Printed in the United States of America

This is a work of fiction. Names, characters, places, and incidents either are products of the author's imagination or are used fictitiously. Any similarity to actual events or locales or persons, living or dead, is entirely coincidental.

Lock Down Publications
P.O. Box 944
Stockbridge, GA 30281
www.lockdownpublications.com

Like our page on Facebook: Lock Down Publications
www.facebook.com/lockdownpublications.ldp

Stay Connected with Us!

Text **LOCKDOWN** to 22828 to stay up-to-date with new releases, sneak peaks, contests and more…

Like our page on Facebook:
Lock Down Publications

Join Lock Down Publications/The New Era Reading Group

Visit our website:
www.lockdownpublications.com

Follow us on Instagram:
Lock Down Publications

Email Us: We want to hear from you!

Dedication

This one is for Kelly Johnson over at Lowell C.I. women's prison. You are not forgotten, my love, though it has been a long time. Keep your head up and stay strong. You are not alone. We came up together since Stewart Street Elementary, and although our freedom separates us, we are still all we got. I still believe in you, Kelly. You are still one of Quincy's most precious black Queens. Peace. I got you no matter what.

Ira B.

Killaz On Stand By 2

Chapter 1

Heather damn near fell into the hospital room with how desperately fast she was trying to get the door open. The moment she looked up, she saw the room filled up with children. Desiree's whole homeroom class was present, and there was so much cake and ice cream and noise that she couldn't hear herself think. Somehow, Ella Mae managed to squeeze her wide hips through the bunch and beckoned Heather outside.

"Heather!" Desiree shouted over the noise, waving her hands over her head, trying to get Heather's attention.

Heather turned back, blew the girl a kiss, and got the hell up out of there. Ella Mae grabbed her hand and led her a little way down the hallway, just far enough to be out of earshot.

"What's going on up there?" asked Heather.

The old lady shook her head in frustration.

"That child's teacher pulled a 'Get Well' surprise party for her. And she brought all those BeBe kids along with her,"

Ella Mae said, rolling her eyes. "Don't you know one of those little boys tried to stick his hands down my bosom?"

Heather's eyes widen in astonishment.

"I almost broke his jawbone."

"You hit him?" Heather gasped in horror.

"I shoulda," Ella Mae said, adjusting her large breasts, her pink *Cancer Free* T-shirt rising slightly. She had an irritated look on her face.

"Is that why you called me? You said it was urgent, Mama. What is the emergency?"

"Your brother," Ella Mae said.

Heather blinked twice, confused. "My brother?"

"Yes, baby. Your brother is alive."

Ella Mae repeated what Roland had told her during his visit, her voice steady. The words hit Heather like a punch to the gut, so unexpectedly profound that her knees felt weak beneath her. "Where is he now, Mama?"

"He had some things to do, but he promised me he'll be back later."

"But what if he doesn't come back?" Heather whined.

Patting her hand soothingly, Ella Mae said, "He's coming back, my child." Her faith was unshakable, pure.

"I wanna see my brother."

"You will."

To hear that her brother was alive scared Heather. Should she keep hope alive? Should she let herself believe it? Ten long years had passed—she had attended his funeral! How could this be possible? The only person she knew that allegedly did some shit like that was Tupac Shakur.

But wasn't working with the feds a death sentence in the streets? Heather couldn't help but wonder: What if somebody found out about it? Wouldn't they kill him for sure next time? No doubt about it—Roland would be as good as dead.

"I just can't believe it," Heather said.

"And he said he will notify Naomi and the girls about it on his own terms," Ella Mae added.

"So he hasn't seen them yet?"

"No."

"But he knows what's going on with them?"

"I told him everything—*everything* about everything, and he wasn't so happy about it," Ella Mae said, her voice firm.

"Not everything," thought Heather. Her mother couldn't possibly have told Roland *everything*. She hadn't seen what Heather saw last night, outside her house. She didn't really know the gruesomeness of her granddaughter's behavior out there in the streets, only what Moya wanted her to know.

"Please, God, let him come back," Heather whispered.

"He will," her mother reassured her.

A loud commotion erupted up the hall toward Desiree's room, and both women hurried in that direction. When they finally reached the room, Ella Mae's face twisted in disgust at the sight of Wanda. The evil woman was back—and this time, she had reinforcements.

"I came to get my niece," Wanda said, a smug grin spreading across her face as four men—relatives, most likely—stood behind her.

The four men looked tough as chicken gizzards, and Wanda's crooked smile practically dripped with arrogance, like she was just waiting for someone to try her.

"You can't take her," Heather said, stepping forward.

Wanda's smirk widened. She pulled out some documents, signed and dated by the honorable judge himself, and tossed them in Heather's face.

"Desiree is mine now. I have full custody. Which means," the bitch snarled, "I can shut this shit down, right here, right now.

"Over my dead body!" Ella Mae snapped, planting herself firmly in the doorway.

"Move, old lady!" Wanda barked, stepping closer. "Now!"

Heather sneered like a venomous snake. "You're not taking that child."

Ella Mae didn't budge.

Wanda scowled, clearly losing her patience. She made a move to shove Ella Mae aside, but Heather sprung like a slingshot, hitting that bitch dead in the eye.

And just like that, it was *all gas, no brakes.* Straight pressure.

Chapter 2

For the past 20 minutes, Zamon had been running for his life. After finding an exit point through the woods, he stumbled onto the next street over. But instead of taking his chances there, he shot across the street towards another unknown residence. Slipping between two more houses, he disappeared back into the woods. The woods were his only advantage until he could figure out a way to get the hell out of that neighborhood.

In the distance, police sirens blared, heading toward the crime scene. Good thing no one knew who he was—at least not yet. When Zamon cleared his second stretch of woods, he was dead tired. He found himself behind somebody's house, fenced in with no obvious way out. For a couple of minutes, Zamon leaned against the fence, his chest heaving as he caught his breath.

A few minutes later, he pressed on.

Zamon climbed over the fence and landed lightly on his feet. He scanned the yard quickly but didn't see anything threatening. Moving cautiously, he made his way through the backyard. It was cluttered with a trampoline and old 1984 Cadillac Coupe de Ville that looked like it's been unattended for years, a few broken bicycles and—

"Oh shit!" Zamon froze in his tracks when a big, black hairy Chow dog stepped around the corner of the house.

The dog stopped, bared its teeth, and charged forward.

"Fuck!" Zamon spun around and took off running back for the fence.

He didn't want to shoot this dog too—it would bring unwanted attention. He had enough adrenaline pumping through him to think he could outrun the dog. At least, he thought so. What he didn't expect was how fast the Chow actually was.

Just as Zamon made the move to jump over the fence, the Chow latched onto the back of his leg. A sharp, burning pain exploded through his body as the dog's jaws clamped down.

"Fuck!" Zamon screamed, clutching the fence for dear life. The harder he tried to pull away, the more the Chow's teeth sank into his flesh, ripping through it with savage agony.

"Stop!" Zamon cried out in desperation." Lemme go!"

The dog snarled, unrelenting, its teeth digging deeper into his leg. Letting out a deranged cry that would have made the Devil himself shiver, Zamon released his grip on the fence and reached for his gun. He fumbled for the weapon, his vision blurred with pain. Just as he was about to blow the dog's brains out, the Chow suddenly released him, and latched onto his gun hand.

The gun went off, sending a bullet flying wild. The sharp crack of the shot startled the dog, which immediately let go and backed off. It gave Zamon a strange, almost human-like look before turning tail and running away at the sound of a young boy calling out, "Bear! Bear!" The dog disappeared around the corner as the boy peeked out the back door. When he saw Zamon lying there, bloody and broken, the kid shot back inside screaming for his mother.

Zamon was in so much pain he couldn't move. His leg throbbed like it was on fire, and his hand was swollen and mangled. He was completely fucked up.

A moment later, the boy's mother burst through the back door. She stopped dead in her tracks when she saw Zamon sprawled out near the fence, her face contorted in pure horror.

"Oh my gawd! I'm sorry! I'm so sorry!" she cried, running to his side. She knelt down and inspected his wounds with shaking hands. "Can you stand? Let me help you. C'mon, I won't let you fall," she assured him as she hooked his good arm over her shoulders.

The trek back to the house across the backyard was long and excruciating. The Chow—Bear, as the boy had called it—pranced around like everything was all good, wagging its tail as if it hadn't just mangled a man. Zamon glared at the dog, his jaw clenched. He wanted to kill that fucking dog.

The boy's mother, who introduced herself as KeKe, helped Zamon through the bathroom door and set him down upon the commode. She quickly got to work gathering up supplies to clean and bandage his wounds. A moment later, after KeKe had gone to do something, the little boy appeared in the bathroom doorway with a sullen expression on his face.

"Thank you, sir," said the boy.

"For what?' Zamon winced, the pain radiating through his arm and leg.

"For not shooting Bear," the boy said, pulling something from behind his back. It was Zamon's gun.

"I love my dog," the boy added, holding the gun out to him.

Zamon stared at his gun, momentarily stunned. He had been so preoccupied with the pain that he hadn't realized he'd left the gun behind.

When KeKe returned, she froze when she saw the gun in her son's hands. She looked at Zamon, her eyes filled with both alarm and suspicion. Without a word, Zamon took the gun from the boy, turned, and tossed it into the trash can.

"That's better?" he asked, looking at KeKe.

"Yes," she said simply, her voice tight.

KeKc resumed tending to Zamon's injuries with focused determination. Zamon sat quietly, the boy's words playing in his mind: *"I love my dog."*

He glanced at his shredded leg and arm and thought bitterly, *I don't love the dog.*

Daisy was on her way back from a delivery when she cruised to a stop behind a thirteen-car backup. She didn't have time for this shit. She had five more orders to fulfill. But something up ahead caught her eye. Her stomach sank when she recognized a car being towed off the road. It looked just like Joya's car. As the traffic inched forward, Daisy's heart dropped. It was Joya's car!

"Noo!" Daisy screamed, banging the steering wheel as her eyes locked onto the ruined car.

The car's front passenger side was crushed all the way to the engine, folded like a crushed soda can. Daisy swung her car to the side of the road behind the mangled car. She got out and ran over to Joya's car, peering inside.

"Hey, lady, what're you doing?" said the driver of the tow truck, who had decided to park the car on the side of the road for some strange reason.

Daisy didn't pay the man no mind as she reached for her cellphone to call the bakery.

No answer.

"What happened?" Daisy asked the truck driver guy.

He hung his lean upper torso out the window of the truck to look back at her. When he told her about the car swerving into incoming traffic, Daisy felt the breath leave out of her. The thought of what may have happened to her cousins hit her like a ton of bricks.

Daisy hopped back in her car and sped away, heading straight for the emergency room. There was nowhere else they could have been taken except there. On the way to the hospital, Daisy tried the bakery's phone again, forgetting the fact that her mother had a cell phone. This time, her mother answered, and Daisy rang the alarm.

"I'm on my way to the hospital now," she said.

"Us too!" her mother said.

"Who's gonna watch over the bakery, Mama?"

"Fuck the bakery!" said Cookie.

Fuck it then, thought Daisy as she raced towards the hospital in a panic.

Once there, she rushed towards the information desk, where a pretty brown-skinned female sat staring into the screen of a laptop. Daisy's eyebrows furrowed in silent anger at the woman who was clearly ignoring her presence. That shit had Daisy seething.

"You don't hear me fucking talkin' to you, bitch!" Daisy hissed, slapping a palm down onto the desktop.

That got the woman's attention. She looked up at Daisy with a stern expression.

"Now you see me?" Daisy scowled.

"Bitch?" said the female behind the desk whose name tag read *T. Moore.*

Her hazel brown contact lenses glinted with unmistakable fury now.

"Look," said Daisy, trying to calm herself just enough to get what she needed. "There was a car accident a minute ago, where two twin sisters were brought in. Their names are Toya and Joya Scott. Can you please tell me the status of their conditions?" she asked.

"You stand there and call me out my name on some disrespectful shit, and now you're asking me to help your ass? Bitch, please!" T. Moore rolled her eyes.

Just when Daisy was about to snatch her ass across the desk, another voice behind her intervened.

"I know who you're talking about."

Daisy turned at the voice and saw that it was a guy who had spoken—a fittingly good-looking guy with deep waves and a perfect mouth. She looked into his eyes and saw worry in them.

"Please tell me they are okay," Daisy said, her tone desperate.

"They're still alive," he said. "Doctor Feldstein had them both rushed into surgery, so that's where they are right now. You're their cousin Daisy, right?"

"How do you know?" she asked quickly.

T. Moore stared daggers into the back of Daisy's head. Suddenly, Cookie and Naomi came running into the emergency room, heading straight for Daisy. How they got there so fast, one will never know.

"Where are they?' Naomi demanded.

"Come with me," said the guy. "I'll show you where they are." He turned to lead the way.

"You can't take them back there!" T. Moore protested.

"Shut up, Tamika!" he said.

"Yeah, bitch," Daisy snarled. "Shut the fuck up before your ass ends up back there too!" she spat, following her mother and aunt as they raced towards the operation room.

When Moya pulled up with her Youngins, they came three cars deep. They parked outside Tron's house behind his car. Moya got out of the car and headed for the front door just as Tron stepped out onto the front porch.

"Where the muthafucka at?"

"He ain't here," said Tron. "He haul ass!"

"And you let him leave?" Moya said.

Tron shrugged.

Moya took the four steps up to the porch to stand before her young goon. They both stared into each other's eyes, and Moya would swear she saw something strange in his.

"Why was Roland here at your house, Tron?"

"Because," Tron said, "he's my father."

His response was the last thing Moya expected to hear. Something shadowed in her eyes, and Tron felt he knew what it was. She thought he was bullshitting with her.

"Repeat what you said, Tron," she said.

"Roland is my father, Mo'. But I don't respect the nigga for what he did to me."

"Tron…" Moya looked deeply at him now, recognizing the resemblance and reaching up to touch his face.

She had no idea this was possible, for she hadn't really looked at him the way she was now. There was no doubt this was Roland's son. Then, before she even realized what she was doing, she had forced him back against the front door with her hand around his throat. The rest of the Youngins just looked on.

"You knew this shit all along, nigga? How could you!" Moya growled like a mean Rottweiler.

"I didn't know! I found out today—just now!" Tron said.

"Liar!" she squeezed tighter.

"No, I'm not!" he said.

Then Tron grabbed her arm and forced her to let him go. Now he was really mad as he got up in her face, breathing hard, chest heaving repeatedly.

"I'll never fuckin' lie to you! When I got here, that nigga was sittin' in my goddamn house bringing up old shit like it mattered to me."

"Tron?" Moya replied after a long moment.

"What!" he replied aggressively.

"You my muthafuckin' brother," she said softly. "I can't believe it. All this time you've been my little brother. That pussy nigga was really busy, huh?"

Tron shook his head wearily.

"Step out here with me for a minute," Moya said, noticing Tron's mother peeking through the window curtains next to the front door.

As they shifted over into the front yard, Tron told her in detail what had actually transpired between him and Roland before she came. A car passed by along the street as all sight of Moya's shooters maintained their positions. At the slightest whiff of danger, the guns were coming out.

"You don't have to be part of this shit if you don't want to, Tron," said Moya.

"What the hell are you saying, Mo'?" he frowned.

"You better quit bowing up at me before I drop your ass. Don't get this shit twisted, boo. I'll still break your ass off something proper," she warned him. The next time he got all up in her grill, she was gonna bust his fucking head, brother or not.

Her cell phone rang, but she ignored it.

"Like I was saying," Moya continued.

"I don't give a fuck about that nigga, Mo'. Whatever you choose to do, I'm down wit' it. We ride together, we die together," he said, extending his fist for some love.

"That's what the fuck I'm talkin' 'bout!"

"And Mo'?" he said, as the skies darkened overhead.

She looked at him expectantly. "Yeah?"

"You my muthafuckin' sister!" he grinned. "Now them muthafuckaz really got hell on their hands."

Moya nodded with a smirk. She had always wanted to know what it actually felt like to have a little brother. Now she had one. What was this world coming to?

Chapter 3

Ella Mae finished reading the legal documents Wanda had provided and tossed the papers in the air. She couldn't believe what had just happened, and there wasn't a damn thing she could do about it, especially after Wanda had threatened to file a restraining order against both her and Heather. The bitch was playing a dirty game. Getting back into that room now meant going to jail in the process. They underestimated Wanda. They thought they had gotten away. Ella Mae would have never expected her to take the matter all the way to the courts.

Ella Mae wanted to so bad to call Moya, but she was afraid her granddaughter would shut the whole hospital down. There was no doubt in her mind Moya would snap— both Toya and Joya as well.

"I can't believe this foolishness!" said Ella Mae as she and Heather now occupied the hospital's waiting room.

"Could they actually get away with that?" asked Nurse Tabitha Knox, a short, thick red bone chick that Heather knew personally. "I mean she isn't biologically kin to the girl."

"Her having Brodrick's last name killed it. He signed off on her birth certificate, and now this bitch done got his permission and signature to take full custody of Desiree." Heather shook her head sadly, her lip busted, and the small cut along the cleft of her chin bandaged.

"There must be something we can do," said Ella Mae. "I can't give up on that child."

"Me neither."

The nurse chick said, "Why don't you take her home so she can get some rest?"

The tired and weary look she saw and the old lady's eyes worried her. That's why she asked Heather to do such a thing. Her mother needed rest.

"There isn't much we can do right now anyway."

Heather looked at her mother and saw exactly what the nurse saw. She didn't like to see her mother look so dejected, with her head in her hands and her heart heavy with the loss of that poor little girl's presence. It hurt to know that Wanda had won, and that Desiree was forced to deal with her.

"What're yall doing out here?" said Vonda, who suddenly appeared and gave the nurse an excuse to leave. "And why y'all lookin' all down and stuff?"

"She took Dez away from us," Heather looked up.

"She who?"

"That dirty bitch Wanda."

Vonda gasped "What happened to your face?"

Heather frowned. "That dirty bitch made me drag her ass just now," she said.

"Take me home, Heather," said Ella Mae.

"Okay, Mama!" Heather rose to her feet in a hurry as she turned towards her mother to help her up.

In the process, she gave Vonda a brief explanation of what went down a minute ago back at the room.

"That's fucked up," said Vonda with a sour look on her face.

She stared in the direction of Desiree's room was and pondered her next move.

"Okay," she nodded. "That bitch wanna play creep. I got something for that ass."

"Don't go getting in any trouble, child," Ella Mae said to Vonda.

"I'm not, Ella Mae. I'm good at what I do."

"Just be careful, girl," said Heather.

"Trust me," Vonda said. "I'm very careful."

He hadn't gone far at all—just enough distance to see what had happened when Moya arrived. What Roland had just witnessed stole his breath away. Everything he'd been told about his daughter was presented to him in vivid detail. Roland was totally dumbfounded. He was so amazed it made his heart skip a beat. His daughter was a gangster for real.

But what astonished him the most was how she ran her team. He liked how they all exited the cars first, surveying their surroundings before she got out. Then he liked how her shooters put space between them, standing guard and watching everything that moved. Roland was very impressed by their smooth, systematic formation. Even the Homeland Security would have to give props to how Moya's young goons protected her.

And then it began to rain outside.

Was that a sign, an omen? Roland thought.

When Moya and her crew left without further incident, Roland came out of hiding. He ran hard for his car and took off after them, trying to see where they were going. He didn't catch up to them until they were already about two blocks away.

After about fifteen minutes of following them from a safe distance, Roland noticed he wasn't the only one tailing them. The car he thought was just staying back cautiously was, in fact, hanging back on purpose. It was following Moya, just like he was. Roland found himself wondering why the car was lagging so far behind. Now, he needed to know just who this was on his daughter's tail.

What the hell was going on?

Suddenly, a red light up ahead brought the line of cars to a stop. To Roland's disappointment, the first two cars in Moya's motorcade continued through the light, while the rear car stayed behind. That's when Roland saw one of Moya's shooters bolt out of the car with an AR-15.

The shooter ran up to the car in front of Roland's and let it rip, spraying the vehicle mercilessly with bullets before running back to his car and speeding away.

"Gotdamn!" Roland exclaimed out loud, having just witnessed a cold-blooded murder right before his eyes.

It wasn't that he was scared—the move was just unexpected. He damn sure didn't see that coming. And what made Roland even more appalled was the fact that the shooter was his very own son. The low-fitted cap and sunglasses did nothing to disguise who he was. Roland recognized Tron immediately from the clothes he was wearing.

"Damn, son." Roland bust a U-turn. "You the truth!" he said as he distanced himself from the scene.

If only Lisa knew what he'd just done, she would probably look at him differently than just her baby boy. She would no doubt lose her mind. She didn't even know—but Roland did. Lord knows he did…

Their son was a stone-cold killer.

***

Bear was barking nonstop outside, as if he knew what was going on in the house. And that was Zamon laid up in the living room on the couch, his bandaged leg elevated and his wounded arm draped over his stomach. KeKe had done a damn good job cleaning his wounds and performing like a medical doctor, especially for her not to be one. KeKe and little Malcom were a godsend. If it wasn't for them, Bear probably would have ripped him to pieces. Zamon had never been so grateful in his life.

"Now would you please tell me what were you doing in my backyard, Amani?" said KeKe, entering the room after taking a quick shower and cleaning the bathroom floor.

She was not a beautiful woman, nor was she ugly, but she most certainly had a body of an hourglass. KeKe had sex appeal. She was different.

"I was running away from somebody and had to jump the fence behind your house," he admitted, having so far only lied to her about his name.

"You had come from outta those woods?"

He nodded.

"Who was chasin' you?" she asked.

KeKe had put on a pair of khaki shorts and a tank top that complimented her smooth, round shoulders and her walnut complexion. She was in very good shape, obviously accustomed to exercising and maintaining her weight.

Zamon winced when he moved to sit up, causing KeKe to rush to his aid.

"I'm good," he told her.

He, too, was in a white tank top.

"I don't know who those clowns were that was after me."

Then he went on to explain how he was at a nearby convenience store and bumped into some guys who thought he was from somewhere else.

"I told them I was from out of town visitin' a friend," he said.

"Bad move," said KeKe.

"They tried to jump me, so I ran."

"But you have a gun?"

"All guns aren't meant to be used in certain situations," said Zamon, being careful not to move his arm.

She nodded.

"So where you from, Amani?"

"Georgia," he said.

"So you're a Georgia peach, huh?" KeKe smiled.

"I wouldn't say all that," he said. "More like a candy apple."

"Mmm," she licked her lips. "My favorite."

Chapter 4

The bathroom door opened, and Wanda stepped out with an ice pack over her right eye. Her eye was nearly swollen shut. Added to her injuries was a busted nose, a split lip, and multiple bruises along her face, neck, and arms. Heather had really done a number on her, leaving the bitch no room to talk. Even worse was the fact that her two brothers, uncle, and cousins did nothing to help her while Heather was beating her ass. They literally stood there like a bunch of bitches. Of course, the whole purpose of them being present was to protect her, and they couldn't even do that. So Wanda cussed their asses out and told them to leave. She was so emotional that the doctor threatened to sedate her ass. Her brother Tim, her cousin Doug, and cousin Keith were still there rolling with her while the others left.

Checking the time and seeing that it was a little after four, Wanda looked toward Desiree's bed and found it empty. The girl was standing in the corner of the room with a dark scowl on her face, watching everybody around her. Desiree was on point, always on guard, especially now that she was surrounded by four adversaries. She kept her back against the wall. She trusted no one. Wanda gave her a hard look.

"You'll get tired after a while," said Wanda.

Desiree didn't respond. She just glared at all of them. Her legs certainly were growing tired after standing up for almost three hours now. She was a stubborn little something. Hell, she'd been through worse.

A minute later, the door opened, and in walked the nurse in her yellow-and-black scrubs, but this wasn't your ordinary nurse—it was Vonda pretending to be one. At the sight of her, Desiree automatically knew she was up to no good. Especially when she retrieved the mobile blood pressure machine and wheeled it over to where Desiree stood in the corner of the room.

"What are you doing out of bed, little one?" said Vonda, making sure her back was turned toward the others.

Tim and Keith both were locked in on her fifty-five-inch bubble butt while the other cousin slept.

"Hardheaded," said Wanda. "Like always."

"Well," Vonda said as she slid the blood pressure cuff over the girl's arm, "be a good girl and let me check your vital signs. Okay?" She gave Desiree a smirk.

Then she sneakily slipped a folded note into her hand.

I'ma get you outta here.

"Okay," said Desiree, feeling giddiness overwhelm her as she allowed Vonda to do her thing.

After Vonda finally took her leave, Desiree entered the bathroom and unfolded the note. As she read the short message, her heart began racing with adrenaline. Tonight, she'd be rid of her evil aunt's clutches. Vonda had a plan, and Desiree couldn't wait to be gone.

* * *

When night eventually fell, the streets really came alive all at once as everybody sprouted to life after being confined behind closed doors the majority of the day. Ever since it was known that the Feds were in town on top of TPD snatching niggas up for any little reason, nobody wanted any parts of that. Damn sure not Jon Boi, as he brought the blunt to his mouth for a much-needed pull. He was mourning right now in private. His uncle was dead—shot to death at a stoplight while rolling in an unmarked car. Another good reason for the authorities to shut the city down much tighter now.

Jon Boi had just spoken to his uncle. They were planning to utilize these crucial moments to capitalize in the streets right under the Feds' noses. While everybody had their shops closed, Jon Boi was using his uncle to distribute his product. No one would have expected the detective. Rogers was too good at what he did. He was seasoned, but there was one thing that may have thrown him off balance, and that was the resurrection of Roland Scott—the same nigga Jon Boi thought he had killed ten years ago. The nigga's sudden reappearance had become a thorn in his uncle's side.

Could Roland have something to do with the murder? Jon Boi pondered as he sat outside his uncle's house. If so, why would he want to see the detective dead?

Jon Boi knew the story about his uncle and Roland's miraculous first encounter. From what he was told by his uncle, he and Roland were good before the attempt on his life all those years ago. He said Roland knew nothing about their relation. Their being family was under wraps. Regardless of what the situation may be, Jon Boi still wanted to finish what he started. He wouldn't be able to sleep right knowing Roland was still out there. And then there was the Moya situation. He still didn't know how he was going to execute that one.

A pair of headlights appeared behind him as a vehicle turned onto the street headed his way. He recognized his

Aunt Pam's car, and he got out. Before she brought the car to rest in the driveway, he was standing there to open her car door for her.

"The strongest woman I'll ever know," he said.

She allowed Jon Boi to help her out of the car. She then looked up at him and said, "I'mma need more than strength to deal with this alone, Jon Boi."

"Who said you'll deal with it alone?"

"I saw him, Jon Boi," she began to sob uncontrollably. "I had to go in there to identify his body. I don't think I'll ever want to see him again . . . Not like that . . . Not dead!"

The woman fell to pieces. Jon Boi helped her into the house and laid her on the sofa. He stayed right there by her side as she cried herself to sleep. Then he picked up his phone and called his resource.

"Yes," a lovely female voice replied.

"I need some answers," he demanded.

"Oh. Hello, Jon," she seemed alert now after recognizing his voice and hearing the seriousness in his tone.

"I do have something for you," she said. "The video footage from the traffic light only reveals that the shooter exited from a gray Monte Carlo. As for the identity of the shooter, it's still unclear as of now."

A gray Monte Carlo, Jon Boi thought.

"One more thing," he said.

"And that is?"

"Was there another car behind his?"

"Affirmative. A black Mercedes Benz, late edition," she said.

"*A Monte Carlo and a Benz*," frowned Jon Boi.

In order for his uncle to have been killed, someone had to notice that he was following them. That could have come from both ways. This Jon Boi knew because he'd already been there before. Now it was his turn to do what needed to be done. Find young Ray Ray and smash him! He was the only one he knew that drove a gray Monte Carlo.

***

Toya's eyes fluttered open, and instant panicked attacked her like never before. She cried out in pain and agony as her drug-induced brain failed to hide the fact that she was not her normal self. Through the terror she was experiencing, another voice spoke to her, penetrating dark shadows in her mind and commanding her to calm down. That soothing voice was her mother's as her gentle hands began to caress her cheek and hold on to her own hand.

After a while, Toya allowed herself to calm down, but her heart was still beating hard as images of her coming to and going back under several times during her inpatient status came rushing back to her at once. The last thing she was forced to remember was her and Joya riding in her car.

"Twin!" Toya began to panic again. "Joya? Where is my sister?" she cried out as she stared up at her mother.

"Your sister is okay, honey," said Naomi, her own eyes welling up with tears.

"Where is she, Mama?"

Naomi stared down at her eldest daughter was loving her eyes, rubbing Toya's arm soothingly. When she had learned about the accident, she almost lost her mind. All she could think about was whether her girls were alive or not. With Joya succumbing to a broken arm, a broken jaw, and several other minor bruises, and Toya having only endured a concussion and neck injury from the brutal airbag exploding out at her, it was enough to make Naomi drop to her knees. Only God could have prevented the worst from happening.

"Mama?" said Toya. "Where is Joya?"

Naomi snapped out of her reverie. "She's just down the hall, Toya. Your twin is alright, baby. I swear to you she is."

"I need to see her," said Toya.

For some reason, her right hip bone was hurting.

"How alright is she?"

Her mother told her everything she knew of the situation. "Who's with her? I want to be by her side," said Toya as she made an attempt to get out of bed. "Joya needs me, Mama. I gotta be there for my sister—"

Toya's words were cut short as the door opened and Haasi stepped into the room. Once again, her heart began thumping hard in her chest as she sat with a cultivated look on her face. Naomi looked up at Haasi and offered a kind smile. He couldn't take his eyes off Toya as they locked gazes, but he still proceeded with his approach and came to rest alongside the bed in front of Naomi.

"I just spoke with my cousin, and he said that it's possible to relocate Joya down here with her."

"Can he make it happen tonight?" Naomi cut in.

Haasi nodded.

"Let me go tell Joya," Naomi said.

She gave Toya another gentle caress on her cheek and a kiss on her forehead.

"I'll be back, honey," she said and took her leave.

Without a word, Haasi let down the bed rail and climbed next to Toya for a seat. Still, Toya just stared quietly at him, her gaze taking in every inch of him, every mark, every line, and every crease. Seeing Haasi again after all these years still made her heart do some crazy things. He still had that effect on her. The same boy who had once broken her heart.

"After all this time I've dreamed of seeing you again, I'd never expected it to be like this," said Haasi, his voice still a mesmerizing liquid of sound. "But it's good to see you anyway, Toya, despite your current predicament."

"This is not a good time, Haasi," she said.

"I know it isn't."

"When my cousin Jason called me and told me that he was transporting you and your twin to the emergency room, I dropped everything I was doing and came to you." Haasi reached over to stroke her chin.

"Jason? Jason Peacock?"

"Yeah."

"He was one of the paramedics?"

Haasi said, "Has been for almost a year now. After bringing you here, he wouldn't leave your side until he was sure that you had someone here to support you."

"Why, Haasi?" she whispered.

"Why what?"

"Why drop everything and come to me?"

Her question made him look away for a brief moment, then he turned back to face her.

"Because you still care? You still love me? Or because you want to take advantage of this opportunity to play on my vulnerability with hopes of lettin' yourself believe that you could fuck me again?" she frowned as she said this, seeing the shock of her words dance in his eyes.

"I would never take advantage of you, Toya," he said. "Especially not when you're at your weakest point."

"You did that already, Haasi," she said, getting down from the bed. "And this definitely is not my weakest point. My weakest point was when you walked out of my life three years ago."

And that's exactly what she did to him—walked out of the room and out of his life.

Chapter 5

For the fifth time in a row, Zamon tried calling Joya's phone, but still no answer. He wasn't sweating it though. He just wanted to make sure she was good, knowing how emotional she could get sometimes. But on some real shit, even though what she told him about her sexual lifestyle had caught him off guard, he had to respect the game. He couldn't really be mad at her—not when he had not been faithful to her either.

Joya had come clean with the truth, and that shit hurt him. Zamon would have never expected her of doing the things she admitted to. His girl was a hoe—but at the same time, she still came home to him. And she wasn't wrong when she pointed that out. Joya kept his pockets fat, kept him decked out in the latest designer gear. Zamon couldn't deny the fact that Joya loved him. If she didn't, she wouldn't do the things she did. She was just a sex fiend—a wealthy one at that.

Now here he was, hours later, after running off on Joya, lounging around in the home of a woman he barely even knew. KeKe had taken him in, cared for him, and treated him better than he probably deserved. She was understanding, down-to-earth, and as physically luscious as they come—definitely wifey material. But what Zamon couldn't figure out was how a woman like her didn't have a man in the house. What kind of nigga in his right mind would leave her alone to fend for herself and her son's life in this crazy-ass world?

No sooner than the thought crossed his mind did KeKe appear in the kitchen doorway. Zamon hadn't even noticed her standing there until the phone in her hand went off. Zamon looked in her direction and was caught off guard by the grimness in her eyes. Sitting up straight on the couch, he felt a sudden unease crawl over him.

"What's wrong?" Zamon asked cautiously.

She frowned, the hurt on her face unmistakable. "You lied to me, Amani."

"Lied about what?"

"About not using your gun," she replied coldly. "You have the whole damn city lookin for you right now, Zamon. I just got off the phone with my hairstylist, and she told me everything. How could you? I took you into my home—with my child—and the least you could have done was be honest with me, Amani . . . or Zamon . . . or whichever fuckin' name you wanna go by!" KeKe's voice cracked, and she looked like she was on the verge of tears. "You fuckin' lied to me!"

The room suddenly felt colder, the tension thick enough to choke on. Zamon locked eyes with KeKe and saw the pain there. After a long pause, shaking his head, he finally spoke. "I'm sorry," he said, his voice low.

"You did what you had to do, right?" she asked, her tone softer now, though her disappointment lingered in the air.

Zamon watched as she moved into the living room and took a seat next to him on the sofa. It made him very uncomfortable now to have her sitting so close to him.

"PeeWee and his crew . . . they were a dangerous bunch," she murmured, shaking her head sadly.

"You knew them personally?" Zamon asked, his curiosity piqued. "Friends?"

KeKe's face crumbled at the suggestion. "Hell no!" she spat. "Malcolm's father, Rashad, used to run with them before he died."

Zamon studied her closely. Something in her eyes told him there was more to the story than she was letting on.

"Lemme guess," he said, leaning forward. "They're responsible for his death?"

KeKe closed her eyes and ducked her head as though trying to block out the question. "Please," she whispered, her voice trembling. "Please don't make me go back there again."

Her mouth quivered as she spoke, but Zamon could see the pain those memories caused her. But he couldn't let it go. He needed her to go back there—for him. He had to know. Did PeeWee and his crew kill Malcolm's father? The answer might change everything.

Ella Mae had just laid down in her bed when a strange feeling washed over her. Something wasn't right. She paused, halfway through pulling the covers over her shoulder, when she heard a noise. The first bump she'd ignored, chalking it up to her own movements as she climbed into bed. But this second bump—it was different. It was louder, more deliberate, profound, reverberating throughout the house.

Is someone in the house? she wondered, her pulse quickening.

Someone *was* in her house, moving quietly, though not quietly enough. What they didn't know was that Ella Mae's hearing was sharp as a tack, even at her age, and she knew every creak in the floor by heart.

The intruder was coming up the hallway now. How they gained access to her house, she didn't know. But Ella Mae didn't have time to dwell on that. She needed to act, and fast. With swiftness that belied her age, Ella Mae got out of bed and reached for her pocketbook hanging off the closet door handle. Inside was her granddaughter's .40 Glock, still tucked away because she hadn't yet decided what to do with it or where to store it. Thank God she hadn't moved it yet. Good thing she still had it close.

By the time all the intruder reached the bedroom door, after presumably checking the other rooms, Ella Mae had the Glock out and ready for action. Her heart pounded so loud in her chest, she swore the intruder could hear it. Moments later, her bedroom door eased open as she hid behind it on the other side. Ella Mae held her breath as the intruder paused in the bedroom doorway. The bedroom was dark but even from the doorway one could still see that the bed was empty. She didn't even move a muscle; Ella Mae remained still as a dead snitch with his throat slit.

After a long intense moment, the intruder released a frustrating sigh and stepped away from the door. When the old lady heard them moving back up the hallway, she then sprang into action. Ella Mae came from behind the door and stepped into the hallway behind them. All of a sudden the dark figure up the hall in front of her stopped.

"I knew you was in here somewhere," the voice said before turning around.

"What the hell you doing in my house?" Ella Mae demanded, her voice trembling but fierce.

"Is that a gun in your hand?" the intruder asked, a mocking tone in his voice.

"Darn right it is!" she growled, wishing like hell this wasn't happening. She prayed this was just a bad dream, but she hadn't even fallen asleep yet. This was real. Too real.

"Don't make me shoot you," she warned, her voice faltering slightly. The intruder turned fully toward her, and that's when Ella Mae noticed something long in his hand. A weapon.

Boom!

Ella Mae hollered in startled fear as the explosion of the gunshot filled the hallway. She hadn't even realized she'd pulled the trigger. But the man didn't fall. Her hands trembling, she squeezed the trigger again. This time, the shot put him on his ass, sending the muthafucker sprawling onto the floor, but the bastard still wasn't down. He kept moving. "Stop!" Ella Mae screamed at him, her voice cracking with desperation. "Stay down!"

The man refused to stop. Just when she was about to pull the trigger a third time, the front door of the house burst open with a thunderous crack. Then came a voice that made her heart leap with relief.

"Mama!" Roland's voice roared through the house. "Mama, where are you?"

"I'm right here!" Ella Mae cried, her voice shaky but strong. Roland stormed through the house like a man possessed, finally appearing at the mouth of the hallway. His eyes immediately locked onto the fallen intruder. He flicked on the hallway light, and what he saw made him pause for a double take.

Bang lay on the floor, bleeding from two bullet wounds but still alive, barely.

"You okay, Mama?" Roland asked, his voice softer now.

"I am now," Ella Mae shivered, her grip still tight on the Glock. Roland glared back down at Bang, and his expression darkened. He couldn't believe what he was seeing. Bang, the man who should've died in that truck with his homies, was somehow still breathing.

"You done fucked up, homeboy!" Roland said, his tone ice-cold.

Without hesitation, Roland raised his gun, aimed it at Bang's head, and pulled the trigger.

Boom!

He blew Bang's muthafucking brains out right there in the hallway, with his mother standing just a few feet away. The room went deathly quiet except for the ringing in Ella Mae's ears. Roland stood there for a moment, looking down at Bang's lifeless body, then he turned to his mother.

And just like that, Roland was back in the game.

**

They all had eaten the dinner meals that were brought up from the cafeteria. The only catch was that Desiree wasn't allowed to drink from the pitcher of ice water that came with the meal. At least, that's what the note had said when she read it. Now, Desiree knew why she'd been warned. Whatever was in that water had knocked everyone else out cold almost instantly. Desiree sat there, wide-eyed, watching them succumb one by one. At first, she thought it might've been some kind of sick trick, but when Wanda tilted sideways and fell out of her chair without waking up to raise hell, Desiree knew it was real.

Suddenly, Vonda burst through the door.

"What did you do to them?" Desiree asked.

Vonda gave an innocent look. "Trust me, you don't want to know, Desiree," she said calmly.

"But I do," said the girl. "Will they die?"

"No!"

"Well, I hope she does," Desiree shot back, her voice low and venomous.

"Don't do that, little one," Vonda warned.

"What?" Desiree asked, hurriedly climbing down from the bed.

"Don't wish death on people. Because sometimes, it just might happen. Now, let's get you out of here!" Vonda handed the girl a set of clothes, not entirely sure if they would fit.

When Desiree was finally dressed, Vonda inspected her with a quick glance and noted she'd been almost spot on with the size. The clothes were just a little too tight, but they'd work for now.

"These clothes are too tight," Desiree grumbled.

"It brings out your curves," Vonda teased.

"What curves?"

Vonda laughed, slapping her playfully on the booty and said, "All that you got back there! Now C'mon before I leave your ass in here."

They didn't waste any time getting out of there. Desiree could hardly contain her excitement as they made their way outside. Eighteen minutes later, they were flying down Phillips Road in Vonda's Acura Legend. Vonda had successfully rescued Desiree from the clutches of her crazy-ass aunt. The mission had almost been compromised when one of the security guards recognized Desiree. But Vonda, quick on her feet and even quicker with her words, convinced the nigga that the girl had already been checked out earlier in the day. She explained that only a technical problem with the paperwork had held things up. The guard believed her every word, too busy staring at her big, glossy lips the whole time. Niggas always thinking with the head of their dicks—it worked every damn time.

"Where am I going now?" Desiree asked, breaking the silence.

Good question, Vonda thought to herself. She certainly couldn't take her to her place.

She had too much going on to look after the girl. Taking her to Heather or Ella Mae wasn't an option either—because those would be the first places the police would come looking for Desiree.

Vonda frowned, realizing she hadn't thought that part of the plan through. Her main focus had been getting Desiree away from the house. Spiking the pitcher of ice water with date rape drugs had been easy enough—just a few pills, and it was over with. Now she had to figure out what to do next.

With Toya and Joya gone, that left only one person Vonda trusted to take care of the girl: Moya. Moya would put her life on the line to protect children. That had always been her weakness. Vonda also knew that if she dared to take Desiree anywhere else, she'd have to deal with Moya's wrath, and she wasn't in the mood for that.

"I'm taking you to Moya's place," Vonda finally told Desiree.

As she drove, she grabbed her phone and called Moya. No matter where she was or what she was doing, Moya would drop everything for Desiree. The girl was top priority.

Desiree was finally free.

Chapter 6

Moya was just leaving Flame's mother's house after dropping off some money to help her pay for his funeral and checking in on her. Ms. Gina was a strong Black woman, and Moya deeply admired her resilience. Just like Tyree's mother, Peaches, Ms. Gina had taken his death hard but kept herself together for the sake of Flame's little brothers. Moya had given their mothers fifty grand each, which she had vowed to do for all of her Youngins if that day ever came.

As for Pooh, his body still hadn't been found. Until it was, Moya wasn't dishing out any money. Pooh had played himself by not killing Remy off top. What if the authorities applied pressure on Remy and he ratted them out on some retaliation shit? Especially when they were in the middle of a war. So far, though, Remy had been keeping it G. He still had a place waiting for him in the crew—if he didn't fold.

Moya was now on her way to grab some chicken wings from the joint on Providence Street when Spud hit her up, telling her to swing by his spot. He sounded serious. Spud was a true little nigga, someone Moya never had to second-guess, so she made her way to see what was up.

The spot Spud was referring to was his crib, located on Holten Street in the projects. At just seventeen, her Youngin had his own place and was living it up. When Moya pulled up, she saw that Lil Petey and Lil Ron were also there, posted up outside Spud's apartment building, smoking weed and hanging out.

"Okay, what up, boo?" Moya said as she stepped out.

She was dressed in a pair of skinny jeans that outlined her shapely hips and ass, paired with retro Air Maxes and a fitted hat tilted just right. Spud stepped toward her, his face serious.

"It's this nigga Bizkit, Mo," Spud said, exhaling smoke as he spoke. "He's talking this fly shit about how you disrespected him by doing what you did to you-know-who. The nigga actin' like he got some pressure or somethin'."

Spud took the blunt from Lil Ron and took a long pull, the smoke curling lazily in the air.

"Where is he now?" Moya asked, her tone sharp.

She already knew who Spud was talking about and what Bizkit meant. Tito was Bizkit's godbrother, and as Moya thought about it, she did recall Bizkit looking at her a certain way that day. At the time, she had chalked it up to his game face, not anything personal or animosity for what she'd done to Tito's dead body in front of him. But now? Now it was clear Bizkit had some pressure on his chest, and she needed to see about this nigga ASAP.

"He's up in the spot chillin'," said Lil Petey, bouncing on the balls of his feet like he was ready for some action. The little nigga was always anxious for some gutter shit to go down.

"Oh yeah? Up in your crib?" Moya said, cutting her eyes at Spud.

Spud nodded.

"A'ight." Moya smirked. "Y'all stay out here. Let me deal with him by myself," she added, turning and heading toward Spud's apartment.

The three Youngins watched her as she strolled toward the door, their eyes glued to her until she disappeared inside.

"She better not kill that fool in my crib," Spud muttered, shaking his head.

If anyone knew Moya, they knew she just might do exactly that. It all depended on how Bizkit wanted to play it.

***

The Club Moon was gonna be jumping tonight, thought Ray Ray as he lay sprawled across his girlfriend LaShondra's bed, texting back and forth with his big brother, Damian. He wanted to see if Damian was down to hit the club with him. He usually was.

"Lemme borrow your car for a minute, bae," LaShondra said, coming into the bedroom wearing her hip-hugging Apple Bottom jeans, and bare feet.

"Where you going?" Ray Ray asked, his focus still on his phone.

"To the corner store. I need to buy some more blunts and a chaser for that bottle of liquor Mama got."

Without looking up at her as he read his next text message, Ray Ray dug in his pocket and pulled out a crumpled bill.

"Bring me some Starbursts, and put some liquor in the gas tank too while you're at it," he said.

"Keep your money, bae, I got it!"

"A'ight," he replied, stuffing the money back in his pocket.

LaShondra snatched the car keys off the table next to the bed and walked out. The moment Ray Ray heard the front door close, he scrambled out of bed. Sliding his phone into his pocket, he left the room and went in search of LaShondra's mother, Dorris.

Dorris was in her bedroom, rubbing lotion on her thick, firm legs after getting out the shower. She was a heavyset woman, but the kind of thick that turned heads. As she stood bending forward with one leg propped up on the edge of the bed, her thick wide ass was exposed beneath her towel. Ray Ray's dick was instantly hardened at the sight.

"Boy, what do you think you're doing?" Dorris asked, glancing up at him as she saw him standing in the doorway.

"I know what I wanna do," he said, a cocky grin spreading across his face.

Ray Ray hurriedly entered the room and came to a halt behind her. He reached beneath her towel and grabbed a handful of her soft, pillowy ass cheek.

"You better stop!" Dorris swatted his hand away, but her tone wasn't nearly as firm as it should have been. She chuckled softly as she continued to rub lotion on her legs.

"Stop playing now," Ray Ray replied, his voice thick with lust.

"You stop playing, boy!" Dorris said again, but there was no mistaking the heat in her voice now.

Already knowing where this was headed, Ray Ray unzipped his pants, freeing his already hard dick. He rubbed the head of it between her juicy ass cheeks, teasing her.

"Boy, what are you—oh shit! Damn!" Dorris gasped when Ray Ray slid inside her pussy from the back. She reached back instinctively, pressing a hand against his stomach to slow him down.

"Where Shondra at?" she asked breathlessly.

"To the store to get gas and stuff," Ray Ray replied, his rhythm unrelenting.

Dorris hesitated for a moment before letting out a deep sigh, feeling him slowly pushing his tool half-way into her.

"Okay," she said, putting put her foot down and leaning forward to place her hands on the bed, bending over further.

"Hurry up and tear it up before she comes back. Gimme that young dick, boy!"

"Say no more," Ray Ray growled, grabbing her waist as he began pounding into her hard and fast.

Dorris met his thrusts with equal intensity, throwing it back at him. She was one of them loud bitches when she fucked, but little did she know someone was watching them the whole time.

Ray Ray was unaware that a threat was lurking nearby until it crept behind him and bashed him in the back of the head with a pistol. He collapsed onto Dorris and the bed beneath them.

Dorris screamed and turned to look over her shoulder, her eyes widening in terror when she saw Jon Boi standing there with two armed goons flanking him.

"What the fuck y'all want, man?" Ray Ray groaned, his head spinning as he tried to lift himself off the bed.

Jon Boi stepped forward, his pistol gleaming under the dim light of the bedroom. "I want some answers, Ray Ray," he said coldly.

"Answers to what?" Ray Ray spat, his eyes narrowing into a dark glare.

Jon Boi's sneer deepened as he thought about his uncle— dead and buried. The memory filled him with rage. He was here for answers about who really killed his uncle, and if Ray Ray didn't cooperate, he'd send him to meet his maker right then and there.

***

Back in the Holten Street Projects, Bizkit was lounging in a La-Z-Boy recliner, puffing on a Black & Mild while scrolling through his Facebook feed. At the sound of the front door creaking open, he glanced up and saw Moya stepping inside.

Quickly, Bizkit stood up, his posture stiffening. The look on her face was grave as she shut the door behind her and made her way toward him.

"What's up, Bizkit?" she said.

No reply.

Moya stopped in front of him, her eyes locked onto his.

"You got some pressure on your chest with me, youngin'? Huh?" she pressed.

Bizkit just shrugged.

"If you got a problem with me, nigga, then speak up. Don't be no bitch and talk behind my back. What I did to that pussy-ass nigga Tito, I'll do the same to you—"

Before she could finish, Bizkit's fist connected with her mouth, snapping her head back. She staggered but didn't go down. Instead, she wiped her mouth, looked up at him coldly, and rushed him with a flurry of punches.

Bizkit didn't back down—female or not. For the next few minutes, they tore that bitch up, wrecking the whole room. Bizkit kept talking shit the whole time, demanding respect, while Moya held her ground, giving as good as she got. They went toe-to-toe until exhaustion hit them both.

Eventually, Bizkit slumped against the wall near the entertainment center, chest heaving, his black eyes boring into Moya's. She perched on the arm of the sofa, trying to catch her breath. After a moment, she rose to her feet, pulled her pistol, and walked slowly toward him.

Bizkit didn't even flinch when she aimed it at his head, biting her bottom lip in anticipation. For a long moment, they just stared at each other.

"You know what?" Moya finally said, lowering the pistol. "I respect you, youngin'. I ain't mad at you. You did exactly what you were supposed to do when a bitch comes out her mouth sideways. I gotta respect that."

"You knew that was my godbrother, Mo'," Bizkit said, his voice tight with emotion.

She nodded. "Yeah, I knew. Just like you knew I was gonna fuck his ass up—dead or not."

"No, I didn't. You only said you was gonna go see the body, not do what you did. That shit fucked me up, Mo'. Watching you cut his fuckin' heart out…" Bizkit trailed off, shaking his head.

Moya's tone was ice-cold. "What's done can't be undone. Tito sold his soul to the enemy to bring me down. But I'm a muthafuckin' monster, Bizkit. When have you ever known me to play fair? Yeah, that's my bad for doin' that shit in front of you, but you could've left out."

Bizkit's eyes softened. "I'll never leave your side, Mo."

Moya smirked. "That's what Tito said."

Bizkit frowned. "Do I look like Tito to you?"

"A little," she teased with a sly grin.

"Fuck you!" Bizkit laughed, and they dapped each other up, sealing the moment with a brief embrace.

Just then, Spud walked through the front door with Lil Petey and froze. His eyes scanned the wreckage of his apartment.

"You two muthafuckas ain't comin' back up in my shit no more!" Spud snapped, picking up his fallen Kobe Bryant picture frame with his jersey in it.

That's when Moya's phone rang. She checked the screen—it was Vonda. Without a word, she took off running for the door.

42

Chapter 7

Heather paced frantically across her back porch, her emotions running high while Roland stood silently, watching her. It was the first time she had seen her brother in ten years—ten long years filled with pain, suffering, and hating God for taking him away from her.

As Heather poured her heart out, Roland wanted nothing more than to pull her into his arms, to kiss her forehead and tell her everything was gonna be alright. But Heather wasn't trying to hear that shit. She was beyond reasoning at that point. Their mother's life had been put in jeopardy, and Heather felt like breaking something. She was pissed at Roland for killing Bang right in front of their mother, assuming that the act had left the old woman traumatized.

What she didn't know was how grateful Ella Mae really was to see her son take a life over her. The only thing that had truly upset their mother was having her sleep interrupted, which was exactly what Heather had done when she went to fetch her. Right now, Ella Mae was sprawled out in the guest room, snoring softly, worn out from the night's drama.

"I need to get to the bottom of this mess, Roland," Heather said, frustration lacing her tone. "I'm pretty sure that man came after Mama because of some shit Moya did."

"I'll take care of it, sis," Roland promised, his voice steady.

Heather folded her arms and leaned back against the porch post, staring out into the dark night. As he watched her, Roland recalled something Doughboy had told him—that Moya lived in a condominium complex where he himself had once stayed.

"Where does Moya live?" Roland asked.

Heather gave him the same address Doughboy had mentioned.

"Why?" she asked. "What I really wanna do is go there and wait for her ass. Be right there in her living room soon as she walk through the door."

"You got a key to her apartment?"

"Yeah, I do."

"Lemme get it." Roland held out his hand.

Heather studied him for a moment, then disappeared into the house to grab the key.

Fifteen minutes later, Roland pulled up outside Moya's apartment building. He got out, entered the lobby, and hopped onto the elevator, heading straight up to the fifth floor. Once there, he pulled out the key and stood before the apartment door for a brief second before unlocking it and stepping inside.

The apartment was quiet—too quiet. It smelled of lavender . . . and something else. *A dog*? Roland thought. No sooner had the thought crossed his mind than he heard heavy footsteps approaching. The sound of a metal collar jangling echoed through the foyer.

Then he saw it.

Monster.

The massive dog with a head the size of a damn boulder locked eyes with him.

"Shit!" Roland spun on his heels and bolted back out the door.

Monster let out a deep, menacing woof and charged after him. Roland barely managed to slam the door shut before the beast's body crashed into it like a battering ram, shaking the frame.

"Goddamn!" Roland gasped, staring at the door in disbelief. "What the fuck was that?"

He couldn't believe his daughter was living with a creature like that. Deciding that breaking into her apartment wasn't worth getting mauled, he rushed back to the elevator as Monster continued to pound against the door, rattling the whole hallway.

When the elevator doors slid open on the ground floor, Roland's breath caught in his throat.

There, standing right in front of him, was Moya.

The moment their eyes met, hers darkened with fury.

"Muthafucka," she snarled.

And before she could react, Roland lunged forward and yanked her into the elevator.

***

The moment LaShondra had turned the corner out of sight driving away in Ray Ray's car, Jon Boi and his goons entered the house.

Just a minute later, LaShondra remembered she had left the quarter ounce of Molly on the coffee table in the living room. She had planned to drop the Molly off to her girl, Ciara, who'd been blowing up her phone all evening, itching to get her hands on it for tonight's club party.

"Bitch, you lucky I got love for your ass," LaShondra muttered, whipping a U-turn.

She wasn't even a block away before she was back in front of the house. She parked, got out, and hurried toward the front door, unaware she was walking straight into some pressure. Shit was going down inside.

The moment she stepped through the door, she froze.

The sounds of commotion echoed from the back of the house. Her mother's shriek cut through the air, followed by a venomous male voice spitting threats about what he was gonna do to Ray Ray.

LaShondra snapped into action.

Both her man and her mother were in danger. Whoever this nigga was in her house was about to feel her wrath tonight. Was he back there trying to rob Ray Ray? Then she heard another voice, and panic gripped her chest.

LaShondra crept into the kitchen, heading straight for the spot behind the fridge where Ray Ray kept his backup gun. She snatched up the .380 automatic and flipped off the safety.

Just then, she heard Ray Ray groan loudly in pain.

Her heart thudded hard in her chest as she spun around the corner into the hallway and moved toward the commotion. She was about to ride for her man.

It was going down in her mother's bedroom.

Peeking inside, she spotted three niggas. Two of them were jumping on Ray Ray while another stood watching. Her naked mother cowered in the corner, eyes wide with fear.

LaShondra met her mother's gaze and nodded.

She raised the gun and took aim at Jon Boi. He glanced back at her and moved fast. LaShondra pulled the trigger—*missed*. The bullet shattered the bedroom window.

The next nigga in her line of sight wasn't so lucky. A shot to the head dropped him instantly.

Before she could fire again, the bedroom door flew open, slamming into her.

"Ah!" LaShondra screamed as she stumbled back, knocking into the hallway wall.

Everything happened at once.

Jon Boi stepped around the door and aimed his pistol. LaShondra ducked as a bullet whizzed over her head. Before she could react, he kneed her in the face, sending her crashing to the floor.

"No!" Ray Ray bellowed when he saw Jon Boi aim his pistol down at LaShondra and shot her in the chest.

Jon Boi bolted out the door, leaving behind one of his goons. Despite his injuries, Ray Ray lunged for the man's legs, tackling him to the ground.

Instantly, Dorris found some courage and went after the dead goon and took his gun away from him. LaShondra was fighting to breathe in the hallway. Without hesitation, Dorris stepped over Ray Ray and the other nigga tussling on the floor. Then she shot the nigga twice in the back of the head.

"You black bastard!' she spat.

But it was too late to save LaShondra.

She died right there on the floor with a bullet hole in her chest.

Meanwhile, across town, Roland was moving with precision.

With the expertise of a true gunman, he disarmed Moya in seconds. He stripped her pistol, dropping the clip, ejected the chambered round, and disassembled the slide—all without breaking eye contact. This had left Moya looking totally dumbfounded. Furious, she glared at him.

"You think I need a gun to handle your ass?" she spat.

Roland smirked. "Seems to me somebody already done—"

Before he could finish, Moya swung at him. Roland weaved the right hook but failed to read the bait and got hit with a vicious uppercut instead.

Stunned, he stumbled back, and Moya landed two more quick punches, one connecting hard.

"Nice," Roland grunted, wiping his lip.

Moya went in on him again. This time Roland was ready, and he managed to use his combat skills to his advantage. Even in the close compartment, it was hard for Moya to land a connecting punch. He had her steaming in frustration.

"You finished?" he replied, stepping away from her.

Moya was seething.

Seeing her up close made Roland swell with pride—she looked strong, beautiful, and grown. Despite their differences, Roland was happy to know that he got a chance to finally touch one of his daughters again, but this one had him skeptical. He was in the midst of the worst one of the three. Moya worried him immensely. She was a killer.

"Let's cut all this bullshit off, Moya. I don't wanna fight with my own daughter," Roland said, his voice softer now.

Moya let out a devious laugh.

"Daughter?" she sneered, then spit in his face.

"You ain't my father, fuck boy! My father would never go against the code. My father was a standup guy, and the nigga I'm looking at right now is a *bitch*!"

Roland's jaw tightened. Anybody else would have had their face broken for that level of disrespect. "A bitch!" Moya repeated with venom.

Roland sighed deeply. "What I did, I did for you, your sisters, and your mother." He gave her those puppy eyes.

"Miss me with that bullshit!" Moya snapped. "You made them crackaz break you, nigga. You don't get no respect for that shit."

"Moya," Roland started, "all I ever wanted was to have another opportunity to be in y'all lives."

"Then all you had to do was do your time and get the fuck out. I know about the twenty years them crakaz offered you, nigga. You worked out a deal to bring your connect down and cut your time down to three years. Twenty years from then you woulda got out and maybe—" she shrugged with nonchalancc. "—maybe I'd still be alive to accept you back."

"You still can, Moya," he replied.

"Never."

Roland's face fell.

"You're dead to me," she said coldly.

"Dead?"

"Yeah," she said with finality. "Because the first chance I get, I'ma kill your bitch ass."

Moya pressed the emergency unlock button, and the elevator doors slid open.

To her surprise, Vonda and Desiree stood right there in the reception hall.

"Mo!" Desiree shrieked, running into Moya's hands.

"Get the fuck out my building, Roland." Moya hissed at her father, and he nodded gravely, stepping out the elevator and heading for the exit.

As he walked out, Desiree frowned up at him before turning back to Moya.

Moya hugged the girl tight, but in her mind, she was already planning to go back for her other pistol. Roland better be gone by then.

Chapter 8

It was going on five in the morning when Zamon felt a hand shaking him awake. He opened his eyes to see little Malcolm staring at him, his face groggy but curious.

"What's up?" Zamon asked, sitting up on the couch with a wince. His arm and leg throbbed painfully.

The night before, he and KeKe had stayed up talking for hours, sharing truths and emotions he hadn't expected.

"You want some milk wit' me?" Malcolm asked.

"Some milk?" Zamon blinked.

"Yeah. Mama said milk keeps your bones strong," Malcolm replied. "I don't want your bones to break from what Bear did to you."

Zamon chuckled, understanding the boy's concern. KeKe had spoken highly of her son, but he hadn't had the chance to really talk to Malcolm last night. KeKe had been protective, saying Malcolm got attached to people easily.

Now, looking at the kid, Zamon could see he was sharp—wise beyond his years. That intrigued him.

"Why you lookin' at me like that?" Malcolm asked, wiping his eyes with the hem of his Spider-Man pajama shirt.

"You good," Zamon chuckled lightly.

"So, you want some milk or not?"

"Yeah," Zamon nodded. How could he deny this kid anything?

"Yess!" Malcolm grinned and hurried off into the kitchen.

Zamon grabbed his phone from the coffee table and checked his messages. Immediately, a bad feeling crept over him when he noticed multiple missed calls from the same unfamiliar number. Four text messages followed.

"What the fuck?"

The texts were from Naomi. Joya had been in a car accident. Zamon's heart dropped, but relief came when Naomi mentioned that Joya wasn't severely injured.

He needed to get to his girl—ASAP.

But Zamon had bigger problems. The cops were looking for him, and so were the Kut-throat niggas, hunting him like a ghost. The only thing working in his favor was that most of them didn't actually know what he looked like—except Dominique, Shannon, and a handful of others who had seen his face that night.

If only he could get rid of them too.

Malcolm returned with two cups of milk, handing one to Zamon before sitting cross-legged on the floor with a sheepish grin.

"What?" Zamon winced, taking a sip.

"You like my mama, don't you?"

Zamon blinked, caught off guard by the boy's bluntness.

"I barely even know your mama," he replied.

"But you killed the person who took my daddy away," Malcolm said solemnly. "Mama doesn't cry about it anymore. She used to cry a lot."

"Do you remember your daddy?" Zamon asked.

"Umm . . . not really. I was four when he died," Malcolm shrugged.

That made him seven now. Zamon had heard Rashad, Malcolm's father, was a respected hustler back in the day.

"I don't remember my daddy either," Zamon admitted.

"Really?" Malcolm asked, eyes wide.

Zamon nodded. "He went to prison when I was nine. I ain't seen him since."

Malcolm nodded like he understood.

In the hallway, KeKe stood listening. She didn't want to interrupt, but she also didn't want Malcolm pushing Zamon too far with his never-ending questions.

After several minutes of quiet conversation and even a few laughs, Malcolm hit him with something heavier.

"Will you help me with something, Zamon?"

Zamon drained the rest of his milk. "Help you with what?"

"Help me take care of my mama," Malcolm said earnestly. "She says I'm the man of the house, but you're a real man. She needs a real man."

Zamon stared at the kid, surprised.

"And I want you and Bear to be friends. Will you stay with us? I promise I'll always brush my teeth!"

And there it was—the twenty-six-million-dollar question.

KeKe held her breath.

***

Morning had come, and the skies were threatening to rain again as Naomi stepped out of the car and entered her house. She didn't want to leave her girls' side, but she needed fresh clothes and had a few things to handle before heading back to the hospital.

Naomi was so pissed at Zamon she could strangle him. She had called his phone repeatedly, leaving several messages. *Did Joya hurt him that bad?* she wondered. *So bad that he didn't care whether she lived or died now?* She couldn't wait to see this clown—Zamon was liable to get punched.

After getting what she needed, Naomi entered Joya's old bedroom to grab her things. Just as her mother had figured, Joya hadn't even unpacked her travel bag. It sat partially open on the bean bag chair next to the window. Something in Naomi's gut told her to leave it alone and grab something from the closet instead—Joya still had plenty of brand-new clothes in there she had never worn. Every time she visited, she went shopping and purposely left a couple of new outfits behind, just in case. She was odd like that—always unpredictable.

Ignoring her instincts, Naomi grabbed the bag.

"Let's see," she muttered, carrying it over to the messy twin bed.

Joya hated making her bed. As Naomi pulled clothes from the bag's main compartment, she heard something rattling inside. Frowning, she searched the middle section and came up empty-handed. Then, unzipping one of the side pockets, she found a pill bottle.

"What's this?" Naomi mumbled, holding up the little white bottle and reading the label.

Big mistake.

One of the worst things a mother could ever discover.

"Oh Lord!" Naomi gasped in shock, clutching her chest. "Please, Lord, don't let it be true. Not my baby! Please, not my baby, Lord!" She dropped to her knees, squeezing the pill bottle fiercely as sobs wracked her body in the middle of the floor.

The fear in her heart cut deep, so deep that Naomi felt like she was dying. Then, suddenly, bolted to her feet and rushed out of the house to her car.

"Naomi? Naomi, wait!" shouted Bobby as he crossed the street over from his house.

This was Naomi's on-and-off boyfriend with whom she'd shared a part of her life since the moment she returned back to Jacksonville ten years ago, but Naomi wasn't hearing Bobby right now. Her mind was solely on reaching her daughter. She cried the entire drive to the hospital.

When Naomi finally arrived, she found both of her daughters in their hospital room surrounded by family and friends. Everybody looked up and saw the wild, desperate look in her puffy eyes. They knew something very troubling was amiss.

"Everybody out!" Naomi demanded.

"What's going on, Auntie?" Daisy asked.

Naomi furrowed her brows. "Everybody get the fuck out this room so I can talk to my daughters! Don't play wit' me right now. I'm not in the fuckin' mood!"

That made everyone scatter like Naomi had pulled a gun.

Both Toya and Joya's hospital beds were positioned side by side. Joya, whose mouth was wired shut and her arm in a cast, couldn't speak, but Toya could. She asked their mother what was wrong.

"This is what's the fuckin' matter!" Naomi yelled, stepping between the beds and holding up the pill bottle.

"What are those, Mama?" Toya asked.

Joya's eyes widened in horror at the sight of the bottle.

"Ask Joya what the hell they are!" Naomi snapped, glaring down at her youngest daughter.

Toya looked at her twin.

"How long, Joya?" Naomi cried. "How long have you had AIDS?"

Toya froze, rigid.

"What?" she whispered. "My twin has what?"

It was true.

Joya Scott had AIDS.

She was dying—been dying for a long time now.

Meanwhile, at the hospital, Wanda, her brother—Tim— and her cousin, Doug, had passed out all through the night from the water spiked with drugs. By the time they woke up and realized Desiree was gone, all hell broke loose.

At first, Wanda assumed a doctor had taken the girl, but when a nurse walked through the door with Desiree's morning medication and questioned the girl's absence, the realization hit hard.

Desiree had snuck out of the room.

They had been drugged.

Doug was the first to point it out. "Yo, we got drugged or some shit," he muttered groggily.

Wanda's head swam. *That sneaky little bitch*, she thought. *No wonder she was able to get away.*

Then she remembered the nurse from the night before— the one in the bumblebee scrubs who took the Desiree's blood pressure and brought them their food.

Wanda recalled the name tag: *Hopkin*s.

"Nurse Becky Hopkins?" Wanda asked Nurse Smalls, pulling her aside in the hallway.

"Becky's been out on paternity leave for almost two weeks now," Smalls said.

"Becky?" Tim frowned. "That sounds like a white girl."

"Becky *is* white," the nurse confirmed.

Wanda and her brother exchanged looks.

They had been played.

Desiree had help escaping, and Wanda knew that she was far away by now.

Wasting no time, Wanda called the cops and sent them after Ella Mae, Heather, and anyone else they were associated with.

"You can run but you can't hide," Wanda muttered.

Today she would go visit Brodrick in the county and tell him what went down. Tell him that his daughter slipped out of her grip with one of the sneakiest moves. While the cops did their jobs after giving her statement and testing the drug-polluted water pitcher and finding it positive of drugs, Wanda took her ass home.

By the time Wanda got home, it was pouring outside. She hated when it rained—it slowed down the shit she needed to handle.

Inside, Wanda met the sullen gaze of her daughter, Porchia. Seeing her daughter's scarred face reignited Wanda's rage.

She couldn't even look at Porchia without thinking about Desiree. That little bitch had cut her daughter across the face with a scalpel and left her needing fifty-two stitches.

But Wanda was keeping her cool—for now. Once Desiree was back home, she would face the consequences. Wanda was going to make Porchia beat the fuck out of her.

"Hey, baby," Wanda greeted sweetly, hugging her daughter tightly and stroking her face.

"When is she coming home, Mama?" Porchia asked, her voice laced with vengeance.

"You'll know when she gets here, baby girl."

Wanda didn't want to tell Porchia that Desiree had escaped.

Heading to her bedroom, Wanda stopped by TJ's room to check on him. Her twelve-year-old son was still knocked out, so she shut his door and stepped into her own room.

She needed her fix—bad.

Locking the door, Wanda retrieved her stash from behind the nightstand. A minute later, she was lighting up her pipe, sucking in the crack smoke. The effects soothed her mind as she laid back on the bed.

"I'ma getcha, you little bitch," she murmured softly.

She hated Desiree's guts.

The girl had made her look like a fool.

Chapter 9

Back in the hospital room, Toya and Naomi held each other as they cried, while Joya looked on in devastation. Her secret was out.

Joya's whole plan of stacking her paper and disappearing to die in private was now compromised. She didn't want to go out like this—didn't want her mother and sister to witness her suffer.

Shame and pain consumed her. With her secret exposed, Joya knew more questions would follow, and she wasn't ready for that. Looking at Toya and Naomi made her want to curl up and disappear. Hearing the pain in their cries created an ache so deep in her chest, she could barely breathe.

She was dying.

And there was no stopping it—not even God could save her now. It was too late. Joya knew she could fall out and die at any moment.

"Why?" Toya sobbed. "Why didn't you tell me, twin?" Her voice cracked with sorrow.

"What could you have done, Toya?" Joya struggled to speak through her wired jaw.

Naomi lifted her head. "Who did this to you? Zamon?"

"No!" Joya broke down, tears spilling freely. "He doesn't know!"

Naomi rushed to her daughter's side, pulling her into a careful embrace.

"Zamon . . . he doesn't know, Mama. He . . . oh my God!" Joya sobbed uncontrollably.

Toya stood frozen, the moment feeling surreal.

"We need to know who did this to you, Joya," Naomi said, her voice trembling but firm.

Joya shook her head.

"You don't know?"

"You don't . . . wanna know, Mama."

"I need to know, honey. Tell Mama who hurt you," Naomi insisted, though a dark undertone hid behind her comforting words.

Joya cried harder, unable to look at her mother.

"Who, Joya?"

Toya got out of bed and began pacing the floor like a worried mother.

The door creaked open, and Cookie stuck her head inside, having just arrived at the hospital. Naomi shot her a murderous glare, making Cookie retreat and quickly shut the door.

A mother's love for her child was immeasurable, especially when the child was in a vulnerable state.

"It was Uncle Tony," Joya whispered.

Naomi and Toya stared at her in shock, their faces frozen in disbelief.

"It's true, Mama. Uncle Tony gave me AIDS."

"Shut up!" Naomi clapped her hands over her ears. "Don't say stuff like that! Please, don't do that, Joya."

"He did," Joya insisted, tears rolling down her cheeks.

"Uncle Tony did this to you?" Toya gasped.

Naomi was on the verge of a breakdown.

Tony Jones—her baby brother, Cookie's twin—had been found dead a year ago with multiple stab wounds to the chest. His murder remained unsolved, though many believed his gambling debts had caught up with him.

Before his body was found in his penthouse, Tony had hit for four hundred grand the night before at a high-stakes poker game. Rumor had it someone followed him home and killed him for the cash. When police found his body, the money was gone.

Tony had been Roland's right-hand man, a bad influence in Naomi's eyes. She had blamed him for Moya's reckless ways. But when it came to his nieces, Tony had been a fool— he would have moved mountains for them.

Now, Joya was saying he had ruined her life.

"Uncle Tony and I went out to eat with Emma and her coworker," Joya said, referring to their cousin on Roland's side of the family. "He was tryna get with her. We all had some wine and hung out. Later, we went back to his place and crashed. Next thing I know, I woke up with Uncle Tony on top of me. He was drunk, and he thought I was Samantha." Joya paused, her eyes distant. "I was still tipsy too, but I couldn't fight him off. Uncle Tony raped me that night."

Naomi closed her eyes, a tear escaping down her cheek.

"How do you know it was him who . . . gave you AIDS?" Toya asked.

"Because he told me," Joya answered.

Naomi's eyes widened in disbelief, but deep down, she knew her daughter was telling the truth.

Joya stared at the ceiling, as if reliving the moment.

"When I started feeling sick, I went to him about it. That's when he broke down crying and told me he was sick." She let out a shaky breath. "My mouth hurts," she groaned.

"Is there anything else you need to tell me, baby?" Naomi asked gently.

"Yes, Mama. I killed Uncle Tony," Joya confessed without hesitation.

Silence filled the room. Naomi dropped her head in defeat.

What more could she say?

***

In another part of town, Moya stepped out of the bathroom just in time to see Monster roughhousing with Desiree in the living room.

Since they met last night, the Rottweiler had been testing Desiree, pushing her limits, trying to establish dominance.

But the girl held her own.

Monster did everything but swallow her whole, yet she didn't back down. The dog had finally met his match, and Moya could tell he now respected her. More than that, he had become her protector too.

A twinge of jealousy hit Moya. She hadn't played with Monster like that in a long time—not since the streets got so hot. And they were only getting hotter.

"Everything you need, you already know where it's at," Moya said, meaning the .25 automatic pistol she had given Desiree.

Last night, Moya had shown her how to handle the small piece, emphasizing the importance of staying ready. *Shoot first, ask questions later.*

Desiree was a fast learner. Moya had recognized the beast in her the night she slashed Roland. She could have hit a main artery and bled him out right there.

"Don't forget about Josh," Desiree said suddenly.

"I ain't gon' forget about your lil' boyfriend," Moya smirked.

"He's not my boyfriend," Desiree replied quickly.

Moya cocked her head. "Then what is he?"

"A genius," Desiree said, rubbing Monster's massive head.

"A genius?" Moya repeated skeptically.

"Yep." Desiree grinned. "He's gonna make me rich one day."

Moya chuckled. "That's what he told you?"

"No," Desiree said confidently. "That's what I told him."

***

On the road, laid back behind the wheel of her 2019 Expedition truck, sitting nice on 28-inch Chrome rims, Moya was still pondering over Desiree's words.

What did she mean about Josh making her rich?

Wasn't the girl too young to be thinking about riches? And just how smart was this little white boy? Moya planned to sit Desiree down soon to pick her little smart brain.

Kids could be geniuses too.

FAMU's campus was unusually crowded this Sunday morning. Moya was on her way to meet up with a professor Joya had introduced her to recently. The man was believed to be a big spender when it came to drugs. *Too big.* There was no way he was using all that product himself. He was either flipping it for a higher price or bargaining it off to trick with some of the college coeds.

Professor William Colomello looked like a certified old freak. Moya was also aware of her twin's sexual escapades with him. It wasn't hard to tell something was going on when they were introduced. But Moya didn't knock her sister's hustle. If Joya wanted to get in his pockets that way, fine— as long as he kept kicking out them bands, he had nothing to worry about.

Moya had plans to make him her personal cash cow, which meant spoiling his ass with product.

"Joya!"

Moya stopped and turned at the sound of the voice calling out to her.

She was just about to enter the school's main library where the meeting was supposed to happen. Walking towards her was a breathtakingly gorgeous dark-haired woman, dressed in a magnificent strapless Oscar de la Renta leather and organza dress.

Who the hell is this? Moya wondered as she watched the woman approach.

"You never returned my call," said Linda Valentina, mistaking Moya for Joya. "But I have a bigger proposition for you than those measly two hundred grand I gave you recently. I've been waiting just for you to offer this opportunity to make millions."

"Oh yeah?" Moya replied, eyeing her suspiciously.

Is this bitch the feds?

Her gut said no. If Linda was law, why intercept her before the drug meeting even took place? That wouldn't make sense.

"Allow me to show you exactly what our future could look like together," Linda said, gently rubbing Moya's arm. Her lovely brown eyes twinkled with intrigue.

Moya stared at her long and hard.

"Say yes," Linda murmured.

When Moya looked at her, she saw *money*—way more money than what the professor could offer. Shit, dollars were raining all around her. How could she say no?

***

Meanwhile, back at KeKe's house, Zamon sat at the dining table, sipping his milk while Malcolm ran outside to tell Bear the "good news." He couldn't lie to the kid and say what he wanted him to say. Zamon didn't want to make promises he couldn't keep, but he did assure the boy that he would stay in touch with him, that he would buy his dog Bear something nice. After breakfast, Zamon had handed KeKe a few hundred dollars to buy something nice for the dog. Malcolm was definitely okay with that.

KeKe stood at the sink, washing dishes, eyeing Zamon with a straight-faced expression.

"What? I got a booger in my nose or something?" Zamon teased, making her smile for a change.

"You handled that pretty well, Zamon," she said.

"I didn't want to lie to him."

"But you'll lie to me," KeKe shot back.

She took Malcolm's empty plate and placed it in the sink. She had toasted Eggo waffles, scrambled eggs, and fried some turkey sausages for them to eat this morning. KeKe definitely knew what it takes to make a man feel wanted.

"I'll never lie to you again. I know that!' Zamon said.

"Then tell me why you're really here, Zamon? What reason are you really here and not with your own loved ones? Why would your phone keep blowing up and you don't answer it? Why are you so sad inside? Trust me, Zamon, I'm not naïve or some dumb broad you could just manipulate. No, not me."

"I'm not tryna manipulate you," he said.

"That's because you already tried and it damn sure didn't work in your favor," KeKe said. "Now please answer my question and be honest with me."

Zamon glanced up at her from the dining room table and saw need in her eyes, a raw need for closure.

"I wasn't just running from them niggas," he finally admitted.

With a deep, painful breath, he told her everything. This was what he really needed—more than anything. He needed to vent. And KeKe was ready to listen.

She knew exactly what he needed. She saw it in his eyes. Boy—did he have a story for her! Zamon didn't sugarcoat a thing. He told her how it was, and before KeKe even realized what she was doing, her lips pressed against his desperately, trying to reach his heart with her own passion. But she didn't take advantage of him; she pulled back long enough to show him that she understood his pain. The kiss was her way of offering him comfort, to soothe his weary soul.

When she pulled back, she looked into his eyes. "You admitted your mistakes," she whispered, now resting across the table from him.

What she really wanted was to give herself over to him, to allow him to take his frustrations out between her legs. Zamon had her burning and aching down there, as she secretly stroked her pussy beneath the table.

"Joya is something else," she said. "But you had a right to do what you did. And still, you have your own errors you must correct as well. Don't be a contradiction, faulting her for doing something that you yourself are doing as well." KeKe wanted Zamon so bad.

"You're right," said Zamon.

"But it's never too late to right your wrongs," KeKe said the moment the front door opened, and Malcolm announced his presence.

A moment later, the boy entered the kitchen and told her that someone wanted to talk to her.

"Who?" KeKe asked, drying her hands.

Before Malcolm could answer, Dominique appeared in the kitchen doorway, her face as mask of restless sorrow.

Zamon acted fast and ruthlessly. *The element of surprise.*

Chapter 10

The Youngins pulled up at *Ghetto Fresh*, two cars deep, with them hammers cocked and loaded. One of Jon Boi's homies was posted up outside, talking on his cellphone. Lil Petey walked right up and smacked him across the face with the pistol. Then, Bizkit and Lil Ron grabbed the same nigga and dragged him inside the building. They came to get some answers.

Ray Ray scanned the place—at least ten people were inside. That's when he pulled the Uzi submachine gun from inside his jacket and aimed it dead at the nigga's face.

"Anybody know where Jon Boi at?" he demanded.

No one replied.

"Okay."

Ray Ray sent thirteen bullets into the nigga's face, splattering his brains all over the floor.

Screams erupted, and everybody either hit the floor or found a corner to cower in. The rest of the Youngins spread out, forcing everyone face down. These little niggas weren't playing. They had already kicked in the doors of three houses Jon Boi was known to frequent. That's how they ended up at the clothing store, hoping to find him there.

"Nobody don't know?" Ray Ray prowled the store like a wild predator on the loose.

"I don't even know what the hell you talkin' about!" said a young female in a miniskirt and fake-ass Red Bottoms.

"Yo," Ray Ray called to Spud, who was standing over the chick.

Without hesitation, Spud put a bullet in the back of her head and moved on to the next victim.

"Anybody else?"

The people were too scared to talk.

"Kill everybody in this muthafucker, then."

Ray Ray stepped over another nigga he knew as Boss Hog and put five slugs through his back. On cue, the rest of the *Bonafide* shooters started dumping on everybody in the place. All you could hear was automatic rounds and screaming. The Youngins were out for blood.

Suddenly, gunfire sounded outside the building. Ray Ray peered through the window and saw Souljah shooting it out with the police, holding his ground like a real soldier. He had been left to guard the door, and that's exactly what he was doing—*guarding it with his life.*

The rest of the Youngins burst out the door to back him up. The four cops laid eyes on them and their assault rifles, realizing their pistols were no match. It was suicide to stand their ground. When the smoke cleared, two officers were dead, one was severely wounded, and the last one tucked tail and ran for his life.

"Let's go!" Lil Petey shouted.

They piled into the stolen cars, racing toward safety. But two more cop cars appeared, sirens blaring. Lil Ron and Tron were behind the wheels—they had to go for what they knew. The Youngins weren't surrendering.

"Hold my legs," Lil Petey told Souljah, climbing halfway out the passenger window with his AR-15, spitting those gangster rhymes at the cops.

Then shit went left.

"Oh, shit!" Lil Ron cussed when he felt the rear tire blow out, causing him to swerve and lose control.

The stolen Chevy Nova got clipped by a passing truck, preventing a head-on collision. The car spun wildly and flipped multiple times before finally coming to rest against a fire hydrant.

"No!" Tron cried out, watching the fatal crash in his rearview mirror. "No! No! No!" he bellowed.

Bizkit and Ray Ray stared through the rear window in disbelief. Spud, riding shotgun, refused to look. There was no question—Lil Petey, Souljah, Lil Ron, and Animal were all dead.

***

Forgetting all about his injuries and everyone around him, Zamon rushed Dominique like a defensive tackle, trucking her thick ass and slamming her to the floor.

KeKe gasped in horror and grabbed her son. Dominique's head banged against the floor hard—knocking her out cold. Zamon hadn't expected that. He stared down at her, then looked at KeKe.

"I didn't have time to think," he muttered. "I got scared."

Malcolm stood nearby, puzzled by everything happening. KeKe said nothing, ushering her son down the hall to his room.

Zamon limped into the living room, retrieving his pistol from under the couch. When he returned to the kitchen, he pulled up a chair beside Dominique's unconscious body. From down the hall, he could hear Malcolm whining as KeKe reprimanded him.

"Get up, bitch."

Zamon nudged Dominique with his foot, but she didn't move. His wounds were seeping through the bandages now, and pain shot through his body.

KeKe returned with an unreadable expression, glancing down at Dominique and shaking her head.

"She's been around the neighborhood," KeKe said. "Dominique used to visit when her friend did my hair on the front porch."

"Lemme guess," Zamon said, "she just happened to be passing through, Malcolm saw her and told her about me and what Bear did yesterday?"

"That's exactly what happened. And now he's in there feeling guilty, thinking he caused you harm somehow," KeKe sighed. "But he'll get over it. What I need to know is—what are you planning to do now?"

"I don't have no plan," Zamon said honestly.

Right then, Dominique stirred awake. She opened her eyes and saw them staring down at her. She tried to get up, but Zamon brandished his pistol, freezing her in place.

"You killed my brother!" she spat.

"It was either him or me," Zamon replied coldly.

He felt trapped, unsure how to handle this situation.

"They wasn't gonna kill you," Dominique said, a slight grin creeping onto her bruised face. "He was more mad at me than anything. But you done shot Twin and Dre, and they Kut-throats. As matter of fact," she chuckled weakly, "I brought two of them wit' me. They outside waitin' in the car right now."

KeKe's eyes widened, and she rushed to check.

"Any minute now, they'll be here to see about me," Dominique said, her hope swelling.

Zamon lunged forward and bashed her in the face with the pistol. Dark rage took over, and he kept beating her into a bloody mess as she screamed and tried to fight back. He knocked her teeth down her throat to shut her up, but he didn't stop. He wasn't even aware of what he was doing anymore.

Dominique had long since stopped fighting, surrendering to his brutal assault, but Zamon kept going. He was a man possessed.

KeKe returned and pulled him away. Blood was everywhere—on the walls, the floor. KeKe went into a full panic.

"What did you do? Oh-my-God! You killed her!" She stared down at Dominique's lifeless body and vomited.

"She's dead."

Zamon wiped his face, his eyes cold and empty.

"Where the rest of them niggas at?"

Without waiting for an answer, he grabbed his gun and headed to the front door, ready for whatever came next.

No longer was Zamon that calm, cool, and collected type. This situation had turned him into a monster.

***

As Moya and Linda got out of the black Land Rover, Moya stared at the large two-story brick structure—Linda's $2-million-dollar home. Not too far away stood the Governor's Mansion, but Moya was more mesmerized by this English-style estate, especially the big, gleaming stone water fountain sitting in the middle of the wide circular driveway.

"This is some boss shit right here," thought Moya as she followed the Italian beauty up the steps towards the front door.

Linda, using her own key—no suit-wearing butler there to greet them at the door—provided entry into the house. Moya wondered if she lived alone.

"I would give you a tour of the house, but I like to get straight to business," Linda said, kicking off her shoes in the foyer.

"I'm down with that," Moya replied, but she really didn't care for a tour of the house; she'd seen enough to know that the bitch was wallowing in cash.

Linda led her into a humungous chef-style kitchen, where she brought out a bottle of 1920 vintage wine and two glasses. She handed them to Moya and said: "Pop the cork and pour us a glass while I go retrieve our future.

Those were her exact words, *"our future."*

Moya did as requested, waiting for Linda's return. She had cut her meeting with the college professor short to come here, figuring it would be best to kill two birds with one stone—if Linda was talking right.

Something in Moya told her that Linda was the real deal. They hadn't discussed business on the drive over. Linda had insisted they wait until they were inside, claiming she felt safer discussing it in the privacy of her own home rather than in the truck, which she hinted could be bugged. She trusted the security protection of her sanctuary—and Moya understood that. In this game, ain't nowhere on earth called safe, not even your own damn house.

"Here I am," Linda's voice called from the hallway, and a moment later, she entered the kitchen with a smile.

But Moya wasn't smiling. Her attention was stuck on what the Italian had in her hand.

"Here is our future right here," Linda said, dropping a shrink-wrapped block of heroin on the counter in front of Moya.

Moya didn't even touch it. She just stared.

"Heroin," Linda said smoothly. "The best quality you'll find anywhere along the East Coast and beyond. This is magic," she added.

"Magic?" Moya asked, raising an eyebrow.

"Yes," Linda grinned. "Magic like you've never seen before."

Chapter 11

Magic.

Moya repeated the word in her mind as she stared at the heroin. If she wasn't mistaken, it was just at a regular kilo of heroin—nothing all that magical about it. *Unless it was about to turn into a million dollars in cash right before her eyes.* Now that would be some magic for your ass. What was so special about this one?

"Before I go further, please allow me to share some history with you," Linda said.

"I know all about heroin and where it comes from," Moya said. "I've studied its dynamics, and I'm very aware of what it can do—"

"But you know nothing of magic," Linda cut in, jabbing a finger down onto the brick of dope to punctuate her point. "Now listen to what I have to say before you jump to conclusions about something that is of no importance to me right now," she added, holding Moya's gaze firmly.

Moya rolled her eyes. "I'm listening. Lady."

71

"Thank you," Linda said.

Then she started from the beginning—when Nicholas Vontelli first discovered his true genius that had changed the game over fifty years ago. Moya listened with an open mind, trying to piece together the picture the Italian woman was painting. After a while, Moya looked back down at the block in front of her with a new perception. *She really did had magic in front of her.*

Linda told her everything—the God's honest truth—so that there wouldn't be any surprises later. She was entrusting Moya with her all, her ruthlessness, and everything she'd built. Thanks to her son, Patrick, she had swiped the throne right from underneath his father. Linda had everything—*the ledger, the product, and the original blue print that was stolen from Nicholas all those years ago.*

After her reunion with Patrick and his decision to banish his selfish father from his life, he equipped his mother with everything she needed to take over the empire.

What once belonged to William Vontelli was now hers. *She was the queen of Magic now*, a name she had personally given the product once she took over. There was nothing like it. It was the same thing the Professor had planned for Roland all those years ago, but this time, Linda was now planning to do the same with Moya but in an honest way.

After hunting for that perfect prospect, she thought that she found it in Joya. The young lady was magnetic—Linda was drawn to her immediately. The whole thing about her paying Joya two hundred grand to snitch out her so-called husband was just a ploy. Linda did that to feel Joya out, and Joya didn't take the bait. Instead, she flipped it and propositioned Linda for that same money. That's when Linda knew she had a winner in Joya. *Little did she know.*

Moya was not about to decline this chance to really be plugged in. Her Youngins were about to eat like never before. *That's all she really cared about— "her babies."*

"Now I have something to tell you," Moya said.

Her mind was fogged up with what she wanted to do now that this opportunity had come knocking.

Linda poured herself another drink. "What is it?"

"I'm not Joya."

"What do you mean you're not Joya?"

"I mean I'm not." Moya stared at her. "I'm her twin sister, *Moya*."

"You're kiddin', right?"

"No."

Now it was Moya's turn to tell her story—and boy, did she shock the fuck out of Linda. She would have been better off reading from a goddamn horror book.

Noah was in church with his mother and little brother when his phone buzzed in his pocket. When Noah pulled it out, he saw it was his father calling—his stepfather to be exact, though at the end of the day, he'd always be his father.

"Excuse me," Noah said, bolting to his feet.

"Where are you going, Noah? It's almost communion time," his mother, Stacy, said as his little brother, Evan, lay slumped against her, fast asleep.

"It's Dad."

That was all he needed to say to hush her up. As soon as he slipped out of the congregation and into the carpeted reception hall near the entrance, he answered the call.

"Yeah, Dad?"

But no reply came. Instead, he overheard a heated conversation—clearly a pocket dial. His father had no idea he was listening in. Noah's eyes widened in disbelief as he caught snippets about Moya threatening to kill him, about having to murder a man last night to protect his mother. The conversation continued, touching on his father's plan to contact Naomi and the girls. And then there was this guy, Doughboy, the one his father was talking to. Doughboy sounded street. A real thinker.

Noah was street too. A thinker too. And there was no way in hell he could just sit back after hearing this. His father needed him.

Noah slumped onto a bench along the wall, tuning in to every word. His mind drifted to the stories he'd read online about the killings going down in Tallahassee, Florida—especially the capture of one of America's most wanted drug kingpins, William Vontelli, the same man his father had schooled him about.

His father—known to most as Calvin Reddick—had told him everything. Roland had shared his whole life story when Noah was old enough to understand. Noah had soaked it all in, fascinated. He studied his father's moves, the way he carried himself around people, the respect he commanded. Before long, Noah had molded himself in his father's image—but sharper, more articulate.

Even though Noah knew his father wouldn't approve of him being in the streets, following his footsteps, the pull was too strong. He was in Newark, New Jersey—where real gangsters roamed. No matter what you chose to be, the streets would rub off on you.

But Noah wasn't a gangster. *He was a survivor.* He knew how to play his position. He had a few gangsters in his circle, though.

"Noah?" his mother's voice broke through his thoughts. She had followed him into the quiet hall, concern etched across her face. "What are you doing?"

Stacy was deep in her faith. She wouldn't have it any other way, dragging her family to church every Sunday. Even after marrying Roland, she kept him in the pews faithfully.

"Dad's in trouble," Noah said.

"Trouble?" Stacy frowned. "What kinda trouble?"

"Enough to make me fly out there and see for myself."

He was dead serious. *Noah was coming.*

***

The room was thick with grief and sorrow. The Youngins sat slumped, heads low, bodies heavy with pain. They had lost four of their own, and that shit cut deep. The whole crew was devastated.

The back room of the car detail shop they were holed up in was their safe space for now. They had ditched the stolen whip after Bizkit put the AK-47 on that cop car and forced it to crash. They all got away. But now the streets were blazing hot, crawling with cops—*not that it wasn't already like that.* Ever since Tito got murked, the whole of Leon County had been a warzone.

Tron knew Moya was about to snap. *Four casualties at once? That was gonna hit her hard.* Ray Ray knew it too—but he didn't give a fuck. *When one goes, they all must go.* Moya would have to respect that.

She had always preached that when it was time for war, there was no holding back. *"Go all the way out until your enemies fall."* And that's exactly what they did.

Spud sat with his head pressed against the stock of his assault rifle, tears running silently down his face. He was hurting so bad he wanted to grab his piece and go full Rambo on the whole Task Force. *The good die young.*

Suddenly, the big garage door started rising. Weapons were drawn in an instant, all four assault rifles aimed at the unknown black Land Rover pulling inside.

"It's Mo," Bizkit said, lowering his piece.

The SUV crept inside, and when Moya stepped out of the passenger seat, they already knew—*shit was about to get real.*

She jumped out before the truck even came to a stop. The driver stayed put.

"What's up, Mo?" Tron said.

Before he could blink, she punched him square in the face. Then she turned on Bizkit and Ray Ray, going off before they even realized what hit them. Bizkit punched back, and that's when Tron jumped in, defending his sister. The room exploded into chaos—fists flying, furniture crashing.

Spud stood frozen, stuck on stupid, watching his crew tear into each other. That's when Linda got out of the truck, and Spud snapped out of it, aiming his assault rifle right at her pretty-ass face.

"It's your position to stop this mess," Linda said calmly. "You're the only one with power right now."

Her words hit Spud hard. He glanced at his fighting crew, debating what to do, but before he could react, Linda moved fast, hitting him with a karate chop to the neck.

Spud stumbled, dazed. That second was all she needed—she disarmed him, firing five shots into the metal roof.

The sharp cracks brought everything to a halt.

"Don't ever point a gun at me again," Linda hissed, then turned to the others. "I know this shit hurts, but this ain't how you handle it. Keep your composure."

"Who the fuck are you, bitch?" Tron snarled.

Linda grinned. "The same bitch with a gun."

Tron eyed his fallen weapon.

"Don't be stupid, brah," Moya warned. "Not her."

Chapter 12

As Roland exited the strip club, making his way to his car, someone popped up on him out of nowhere. It was a face he hadn't seen in a very long time—his younger cousin, Peanut. The last time Roland saw him, he was twenty-six years old and had fallen off the scene. Peanut was Emma's son, one of the young hustlers Tony had recruited back in the day. Back then, Peanut was a go-getter, but Roland wasn't sure what he was now.

"Doughboy said you was back," said Peanut, looking fresh in his Gucci outfit.

He and Roland shook hands as Roland regarded him with silent approval.

"You're lookin' good, lil cuz!" said Roland.

"You too, my nigga. You don't look so dead to me."

"Nah," Roland chuckled. "I'm alive and well."

"But for how long, though?"

Roland was taken aback by his question.

"What do you mean by that, Peanut?"

"Let's get from out here," Peanut said, referring to being in the club's parking lot all out in the open.

He led Roland over to his car, and they climbed inside. From the passenger seat of Peanut's candy apple-green Mustang with white leather interior and triple gold wheels, Roland could tell that Peanut indeed was still in the game. He wondered who was his supplier now. What was his cousin moving now that he and Tony weren't around?

"What happened to the 69 Cutlass you had?" Roland asked.

"It's just a show car now," Peanut said. "I put it up for a few years to let everybody forget about it. You should see that bitch now!"

"Oh yeah?"

"I ain't come to talk about cars, cuz."

Roland nodded. "Right."

"Your name is ringing in the streets, Roland."

"I bet it is."

"I'm talkin' about on some rat shit, cuz." Peanut's voice darkened. "Niggas dirtying your name, saying you're working for the Feds."

Roland didn't reply, so Peanut continued.

"They're saying the Feds didn't show up until you popped up on the scene. Then this bullshit wit' that Italian that got knocked? Your name is written all over that too. So now niggas thinkin' grimey out there towards you right now. Be very careful, cuz. The streets ain't the same no more."

"You say you spoke to Doughboy, right?"

Peanut nodded.

"So, you know my story."

"I know enough to lose respect for you," said Peanut.

Suddenly, a half-naked stripper pranced past the car on Peanut's side, hopping into her ride. The club had to be closing up now, because all type of ass and titties was leaving at the same time. It wasn't supposed to be open today anyway.

"I don't respect what you did, cuz." Peanut exhaled smoke from his cigarette. "But you family, so I gotta put you up on game."

"All I wanna do is see my girls," Roland said.

"And that's another thing we need to talk about," Peanut said, flicking his ashes out the window. "You know Moya at war with this nigga Jon Boi."

"I heard about him. I know all his people over on the south side."

"Do you know he my connect too?"

Roland's face darkened. "Oh yeah?"

"And he fuckin' around with Mama on the side." Peanut's frown deepened. "She don't want nobody knowin' her business, but Tony and Jon Boi was tight before he died. That's how they linked up. Now she all fucked up over that nigga."

Roland's jaw clenched. "So Emma fuckin' the same nigga who tryna kill my daughter? And your ass ain't done shit about it?"

"That's where he been layin' low at."

"But what the fuck are you doin' about it, nigga?"

Peanut sighed. "I don't want Mama to get hurt, cuz."

"The fuck you mean, Peanut?" Roland glared at him, shaking his head in disappointment. Without another word, he opened the door and got out of the car.

He knew what he had to do—since his cousin clearly didn't. It was time he met with Emma anyway. She had something that belonged to him.

Desiree was kicked back, relaxing on the plush leather sofa, watching *Top Shottaz*. Monster lay sprawled across the floor in front of her, gnawing on a red Converse Chuck Taylor shoe—fuckin' it up too. Having been a sheltered child all her life, Desiree wasn't used to watching movies. Brodrick always said too much TV was bad for the mind.

The only TV in the house had been in the living room, where Brodrick either watched the news or sports.

She couldn't even recall watching a movie before— except with her mother, Carla, who loved *Bold and the Beautiful* and TV game shows. And that was only when Brodrick was out back in the work shed. If he caught Desiree watching anything other than something educational, he'd kick her out or make her mother turn it off. He was a mean, controlling bastard.

Now, watching *Top Shottaz*, Desiree couldn't believe what she was seeing. Before that, she had watched *Dead Presidents*, and the shit had her baffled. She'd raided Moya's DVD shelf, looking for something to watch, and found nothing but gangster shit—*Menace II Society, Juice, Boyz N the Hood.* Desiree already had *Belly* lined up to play next. She couldn't get enough of these types of movies.

No wonder Moya is the way she is, Desiree thought. Then she wondered what it'd be like if Moya played a character in one of those movies. She'd love to see that.

Monster stopped chewing on the rubber end of the shoe when he sensed the front door open. He climbed to his feet, his thick gold Cuban link collar jangling loudly as he trotted toward the door. Desiree was zoned into the movie, with the .25 automatic pistol lying beside her on the seat.

When Heather turned the corner into the living room, with Monster escorting her in, Desiree broke out into a wide grin.

"What the hell!" Heather said, astonished.

"I'm free!" Desiree raised her arms in victory, then winced from the pain in her ribs.

She wasn't completely healed yet, but she was good.

"I see that," Heather replied.

With a slick movement, Desiree shoved the pistol between the plush sofa cushions before Heather could see it. Then she got up to hug her, but Monster nudged her aside, nearly making her fall. Now they were fighting for Heather's attention. Since day one, Heather had been there for Monster, and after two and a half years, their loyalty was strong. Next to Ella Mae and the twins, anyone else was dog food to him—except for Desiree.

"You got the whole world lookin' for you, girl."

"I've been right here!" Desiree grinned.

"Yeah," Heather shot back with a sour look. "In the damn Devil's den! Have you taken your medication, or do you even have any to take?" Heather noticed the slight agony in Desiree's face and knew her ribs were still bothering her.

"Only what I got from Moya last night."

"And what's that?"

Desiree hurried into the kitchen and came back with a Ziploc bag holding four pills inside.

The moment Heather saw the bag, she already knew what they were. Snatching the bag of OxyContin from Desiree's hand, she shook her head wearily. *Of all things, Moya gave her Oxy? A fucking bag of OxyContin?*

"You are not taking any more of these pills, Dex. How many have you taken already?"

"Only one, last night," Desiree admitted. "And it had me feelin' like I was floatin' in the air."

"That's because you *were* floatin' in the air!"

"Really?"

"No," Heather said, stuffing the bag in her pocket. "But you won't be taking these again."

Desiree frowned. She wanted to float again.

***

"I don't give a fuck no more! That muthafucka killed my bitch!" Ray Ray snapped, foam forming at the corners of his mouth. "Them muthafuckaz beat me in that house. You don't put your muthafuckin' hands on Debra's son!" He looked at Moya.

"The fuck you lookin' at me for, nigga?" Moya sneered. "What! Nigga, you wanna go another round? I don't give a fuck too!" she snarled.

"It's whatever!" Ray Ray glared at her.

"Lil Petey and 'em out there dead, and we in here on this fuck shit!" Bizkit shouted.

Then he cast a glance at Linda and shrugged.

"What we need to be worried about is them crackaz coming for us next."

"Fuck!" Moya screamed in outrage.

"But bruh," Tron said to Ray Ray. "We gotta lay low . . . all the way low after what just happened."

"Tell me exactly what went down," Moya demanded.

No one said a word, but all the Youngins glanced at Linda.

"I'll step out," Linda said, understanding. "I got a few calls to make anyway."

"Out back," Tron instructed. "Not on front street."

Linda nodded and stepped out respectfully.

The Youngins laid it all out for Moya. As she slid closer to Ray Ray, she wrapped her arms around his neck, pressing her forehead against his. Together, they hung their heads and breathed in unison, mourning their dead homies.

"You handled that shit, boo," she whispered.

"It ain't over," Ray Ray muttered.

"It won't *ever* be over till them muthafuckaz in the ground," she vowed.

One by one, the rest of the Youngins surrounded their queen. Together, they mourned as a family. Tron squeezed Bizkit's shoulder, letting him know it was all love. They were all each other had now. Their numbers had shrunk in the span of 48 hours.

Now it was time to go harder than they ever had before— for the ones they lost. For one another.

"It's time to go hard or die," Spud said. "And I don't wanna die."

Chapter 13

Having told Dominique's two homeboys that she was going to chill out with her for a little while, KeKe knew they would buy it. She knew Boonie and Shyne well enough to know neither of them would suspect her of treachery. But the moment she re-entered the house and found Donminique beaten to death, she panicked.

Immediately, Dominique's cell phone buzzed in her pocket with an incoming text from Shyne. Acting on instinct, KeKe retrieved the phone, pretending to be Dominique, and sent a response reassuring him she was good. Now, hours later, Dominique's body was wrapped in two thick blankets by the back door.

"As soon as we get her out of here and away from the house, we're good," Zamon said.

"But you want to put her in the trunk of *my* car?"

"How else are we gonna move her?"

KeKe hesitated, feeling lost.

"Or unless you want to call the police?"

"No!" She shuddered at the thought. The last time she was questioned about a murder—when Rashad died—it left her shaken. She couldn't go through that again.

Taking a deep breath, KeKe went to get her car and brought it around to the back door as close as she could. Zamon then had her empty the trunk of everything inside. During this whole time, Malcolm wasn't allowed to come out of his room. The boy thought he had done something very bad. He cried himself to sleep, which was fine with KeKe—one less thing to worry about.

"Now wait till night," Zamon said.

KeKe glanced at her watch. "That's four more hours from now." It was a little after two-thirty in the afternoon. "We can't keep her for that long without someone coming to check for her."

"Then we improvise, KeKe," he told her.

"Improvise how?"

Zamon picked up Dominique's cell phone again.

"This," he said, holding it up.

For the next ten minutes, Zamon scrolled through Dominique's call log and Messenger contacts, fabricating a series of texts and call records, making it look like Dominique had been in the company of several different people. That way, if anyone came asking, they'd think she had been with someone else last night—not KeKe. That would take a lot of heat off her. It was a smart move. KeKe watched him work, impressed.

Had Zamon done this before?

***

By nightfall, Zamon hid into the bathroom while KeKe let Bear into the house. She put the dog in Malcolm's room to keep him distracted. Bear would have no doubt challenged Zamon again after their confrontation earlier that day. They needed no hindrances tonight.

"Let's do it!" Zamon said.

With KeKe's help, he managed to get Dominique's body into the trunk. It was so dark behind the house they could barely see what they were doing.

"Now go get your things," he told her.

"Okay."

KeKe rushed back into the house. The hours prior to disposing of the body, KeKe had scrubbed the kitchen on her hands and knees. The whole house now reeked of pure bleach and lemon-scented Pine Sol. All the blood was gone—no sign of a struggle.

Minutes later, KeKe exited the house with multiple traveling bags containing her and Malcolm's things. Zamon insisted it was best to get out of Duval County for a while. KeKe didn't argue with him—she just did what she was told. Zamon was running the show now.

By seven o'clock, they were on the road, leaving Bear behind. Malcolm wasn't feeling that shit *at all*. Leaving his best friend behind? KeKe and Zamon will never hear the end of that move. The boy was *heated*.

"Where to now?" asked KeKe.

"You know the way to Tallahassee?" he asked.

Reluctantly, she nodded. That's where they were headed—with a fucking dead body in the trunk.

Zamon figured once he was back on his own turf, he was good. He'd come back later to see about Joya.

Little did he know.

What was even crazier about the whole thing was that Moya had received a text from her mother, demanding she get there ASAP. Her twins were in trouble, and they needed her presence now. Without hesitation, Moya gathered up her Youngins and hit the road for Jacksonville. The Youngins needed to lay low for a while anyway. They had the city in panic mode—everybody was feeling the heat they brought.

She heard through the grapevine that the authorities were looking for the rest of the crew in connection to the earlier killings. But they didn't know exactly *who* all the shooters were. They just wanted to round them up, interrogate them, and brutalize them on the sly—just because they *could*. Not *her* babies, though, thought Moya. They were already out of town, visiting family and friends in Jacksonville.

Linda had also assured Moya that she could reach out to a few powerful people in her favor. After everything the Italian had already revealed in confidence, Moya had no doubt she could make something happen. That bitch had real power—associates in very high places. Her presence had come at the perfect time.

Rule number one: *Protect your investment.*

As for her father, Moya decided to wait until she got there to break the news. It was obvious her mother and sisters didn't know about his *resurrection*—otherwise, they would have told her. At least, that's what Moya *expected* them to do. She was about to find out just how much they had kept from her.

Once Moya learned about the car accident that had happened earlier that morning, she was *going* to snap. All those hours her twins could've been dying, and no one thought to call her? That was going to fuck her up—especially when she found out about Joya's situation. Moya might just die from the pain alone.

Halfway to Jacksonville, they passed Zamon in a Nissan on his way back home.

"What's up wit' these Duval niggas up here?" Spud asked.

Beneath his seat lay both his AK-47 and a Glock .40—his babies. He refused to leave without them. Moya, behind the wheel of the Yukon Denali, puffed on a fat blunt of Kush.

"No different from any other niggas," she replied. "You'll know a bitch nigga from a real gangster though. But these fools up here don't fuck off! This used to be the murder capital in Florida."

"Until we came along," Ray Ray chimed in.

"Damn right," Moya agreed. "But don't sleep on these niggas."

"Underestimate no man," Spud said.

"No man."

From the back seat, Tron, stretched out, said, "But they respect you, right? 'Cause I don't wanna have to bust one of these niggas' heads."

"A muthafucka knows better, lil' bruh. I got a lot of respect up there. I *earned* that shit soon as I jumped off the porch," Moya said.

She started telling them about her affiliation with the Kutthroat organization and how she put on *hard* for the team. War stories rolled off her tongue, detailing how she became the person she was today.

"Good," Bizkit said. "We can chill up there on the strength of you, Mo."

"You niggas know how to move," she said.

"Just as long as they move correctly," Ray Ray added.

He was itching for a muthafucka to give him a reason to put that iron in their life. They were a pack of live wires, ready to set it off. Jacksonville niggas better step right—or get left with a body full of lead.

***

Meanwhile, Toya lay in bed with her twin in her arms, gently smoothing her hair back, staring blankly into space. Her thoughts ran wild, and her heart was heavy with sorrow. As Joya slept in her embrace, Toya prayed for strength—for her twin to be forgiven for her mistakes.

Naomi was beside herself with distress. The doctor had suggested she take a Valium to calm her nerves, but Naomi chose the comfort of Bobby's presence instead. He had come running the moment she called.

The twins liked Bobby; they thought he was solid. He had been around since day one, and even Moya respected him—though she loved teasing him. They were all tight.

For now, the twins had more than enough support. Haasi had come back, despite Toya's displeasure, refusing to leave her side. Cookie, Daisy, and a few others reclaimed their spots, standing by Naomi, who was too exhausted to turn them away.

Hours passed, and one by one, people trickled out. By late evening, only Haasi and Bobby remained. The two men felt it was their duty to watch over their girls.

Then, the door opened, and Roland stepped inside like Jesus resurrecting from the tomb.

Naomi looked up lazily at the doorway. The moment she saw him, she bolted to her feet.

Toya stiffened, eyes widening in shock.

"Joya, get up!" she whispered, shaking her awake. "Look! Daddy's here!"

"Daddy?" Joya mumbled, disoriented.

When she focused and saw him standing there, her heart skipped a beat.

"Daddy! Daddy!" she cried out.

Roland moved toward Naomi, and she reached up to touch his face, unsure if she was hallucinating. She was at a loss for words.

"It's me," Roland said softly. "You ain't trippin', Naomi. It's a long story, and I wanna tell you everything."

Naomi slapped the fire out of him.

Bobby jumped to his feet, but Naomi suddenly broke down and threw her arms around Roland's neck. Bobby watched, feeling lost. He *knew* who Roland was, and seeing him alive now only made him suspicious.

"I miss you so fuckin' much," Naomi sobbed. "How could you do that to us?"

"I had no other choice."

Toya ran to him, tears streaming down her face. Roland pulled her in tight, fighting back his own tears.

Bobby, being the gentleman he was, nodded respectfully at Roland and quietly left the room, motioning for Haasi to follow him. They left Naomi and the twins to their moment.

"I'm sorry I left y'all," Roland whispered, his eyes locking onto Joya's frail form in the bed. His heart shattered.

"*Joy!*" he whispered, bending down to kiss her tear-streaked cheek. "You are my pride and joy, always."

Joya wailed in his arms.

"What happened?" Roland asked.

"It's a long story," Naomi said, refusing to let go of his hand. "But you need to go first. I wanna hear *everything.*"

He didn't hesitate. For ten years, he had waited for this moment.

For the next hour, Roland told them everything—the absolute truth. The part about having another family in New Jersey barely fazed Naomi. In her mind, he *wasn't* going anywhere now. The twins, though, were astounded at the thought of having a little brother.

But when he mentioned Tron, their mouths dropped in disbelief. Naomi's heart boiled with fresh anger, but she couldn't tell him the truth—couldn't tell him the twins weren't his. It would *kill* him.

And when he brought up his confrontation with Moya, the entire room grew tense.

"Moya should be here any minute now," Naomi said.

Roland shook his head grimly.

"She's not gonna let us be together like this," he said. "Moya is beyond reasoning."

"You leaving us made her that way," Toya replied.

"I know," he whispered.

His daughter was a monster. And the last thing he wanted was to have to slay that monster. Lord knows he didn't.

Chapter 14

Remy stared at the TV in horror as the news reporter stood outside the crash site, describing the deadly incident involving the Youngins and the shootout. He could only shake his head as he listened.

"You see there, Cedric," his mother, Sandra, said. "That could've been you right there on TV."

No reply from Remy.

"Yet here you are, laid up in this damn hospital wit' two bullet holes in your legs," Sandra continued.

She wasn't stupid. She knew somebody in his crew shot him, but Remy wasn't trying to hear all that right now. His best friend had died in that car today. He and Souljah had been cronies since elementary school. To hear that Souljah was gone created a malice deep in his heart.

Remy knew if Souljah had been there that night, he wouldn't be in the hospital right now. Souljah would've had his back and prevented the whole situation from going down like it did.

"And you still gonna go right back out there to them," his mother muttered, changing the channel to some other bullshit.

She was right, though. Remy *was* going back. There was no turning back now. Despite his current situation, the crew needed him. Cripple or not, he was still a team player. He had to redeem himself—earn his respect back and prove that he *could* bust his gun.

That night, during the shootout with Wanky's people, the only reason he didn't shoot was because his cousin, Tommy Lee, was in the middle of it all. Remy couldn't bring himself to pull the trigger when Tommy Lee ran out that house. He had his gun aimed right at his cousin, but in the end, he froze.

Tommy Lee had seen him too—understood the situation—but still upped his pistol and bust at the rest of the Youngins. It wasn't until the pressure turned up that Tommy Lee ran for cover. That's all Pooh needed to see to start clowning him.

Little did Remy know, Pooh was already dead—tossed in the swamp with the gators.

The telephone rang, breaking his thoughts. Sandra answered it, then extended the phone toward him.

"It's Tiffany," she said. "Somebody with some damn sense."

Tiffany was Remy's girlfriend—the daughter of a craftsman and a pastor mother. Sandra loved her like the daughter she never had.

"What's up, Tiff?" Remy perked up suddenly.

"Did you watch the news?"

He sighed. "Yeah."

"I can't believe they all died like that," she said, sounding torn up. "I wish I could be wit' you right now, but Mama ain't having it."

"I know."

Remy respected Tiffany's mother, but the woman didn't want her daughter involved with him at all.

"Maybe tomorrow we can see each other," she said.

"Not if you gotta go to school."

That was another thing about Remy—he stayed in school despite his street rep. People like Tiffany kept him grounded.

"There's always our hour recess," Tiffany teased. "Besides, I got some more school work for you. Mr. Freeman's project exam is coming up, and I'm gonna help you with it."

"Man, I hate Mr. Freeman's history class."

"I know," she giggled. "But you're gonna love this."

"I love you already."

"I love you too, baby."

Sandra grunted in disdain.

"Hmph."

For a little while, Tiffany got his mind off the streets. But once he left this hospital, it was on. They were gonna feel his wrath.

***

The burgundy box Chevy pulled into the driveway of the Piper Street residence. Peanut got out and headed for the front door of the house he had proudly bought for his mother two years ago on her 40th birthday.

Unlocking the door with his key, he stepped inside—only to be hit by the unmistakable sound of the headboard banging against the wall and his mother crying out in pleasure.

"Fuck no," Peanut muttered, cringing.

He could deal with a lot of things—but *not* that. What nigga wanted to hear his own mama getting fucked?

Peanut hurried to his room, snatched his *Beats By Dre* headphones off the dresser mirror, and plugged them into his iPhone. MO3 blasted in his ears while he went over what needed to be done.

Jon Boi was in there fucking his mother, but little did he know—that would be his last nut. The nigga was on borrowed time.

Peanut wasn't no killer—he was a hustler, first and foremost. He had heart. No bitch in his blood. He'd never killed a man in his life, but he *had* bust his gun before. Niggas didn't test him because they knew who he was and who his people were. His rep came from running with real ones like his cousin Moya, Tony, and of course, Jon Boi himself. But tonight, Peanut was about to prove his gangster.

His mother would just have to be mad.

Twenty minutes later, Peanut was in the kitchen, sipping some of his mother's Armand de Brignac champagne, when Jon Boi strutted in—buck-ass naked.

"Oh shit!" Jon Boi jumped when he saw Peanut. "The fuck you doing here?"

"Go put some fuckin' clothes on, nigga!"

"How you gonna tell me what to do in my own shit?"

"Nah, homeboy. *You* got the game fucked up."

Jon Boi raised an eyebrow. "Yeah?"

"This *my* shit, nigga."

Peanut's hand itched to reach for the gun tucked at his waist.

"You know what? Get your shit and get the fuck out."

"Make me," Jon Boi challenged, puffing his chest out.

"You think I'm playin' wit' you?"

Jon Boi sneered.

When Peanut just stared at him, Jon Boi smirked. "That's what I thought."

Peanut shoved him in the chest and drew his gun.

"I ain't playin', Jon Boi."

"Then you better use it."

Blocka!

Peanut shot his bitch ass in the leg. Jon Boi howled and hit the floor, yelling for Emma.

"What's going on?"

Emma came running down the hall, eyes wide.

"Get back, Mama!" Peanut yelled.

"No, Peanut!" she cried as he dragged Jon Boi toward the front yard. "Don't do this, baby! Please don't hurt him!"

"I can't."

Blocka! Blocka! Blocka!

Peanut emptied his clip into Jon Boi's chest, blowing it open.

Blocka!

One to the head to make sure he was dead.

"Pussy muthafucka," Peanut muttered, pulling out his phone to call Moya.

Emma collapsed to the ground, heartbroken.

It is what it is. The nigga had to die.

***

The first place Moya stopped at as soon as she made it to Jacksonville was her mother's house. She had to take a shit, and there was no other place she felt comfortable doing it but there. Meanwhile, the Youngins were laid out in the living room—tired as hell, exhausted. As soon as Bizkit hit the sofa, he was out cold. Spud was right behind him, while Ray Ray and Tron remained on guard. It was no different from the shifts they would put in at the traphouse.

All their asses were tired, even Moya, but her casual dose of Molly she had taken kept her up and alert.

As she sat on the commode doing her business, her phone buzzed with a text from her cousin Peanut. In his coded message, he told her that he had taken care of Jon Boi—that the nigga was dead—and he would explain later.

"Muthafucka," she muttered to herself.

She wondered how Peanut got close to Jon Boi to off him.

Afterwards, she entered the living room and found Ray Ray sitting in the living room with his head down. She walked up to him and kissed the back of his head.

"Jon Boi is dead now, boo."

He bolted upright in his seat.

"What?"

Moya told him about the text she received from Peanut.

"Where's Tron?" she asked.

"Outside," he said.

She glanced toward the door, then back at Ray Ray.

"Get some rest, Ray. We got a long day tomorrow," she said softly.

Outside, Tron was sitting on the porch steps, puffing a blunt and watching the streets. She told her brother what the deal was with Jon Boi and what she had to go do.

"Go in there and get some sleep."

"Not right now," he replied, exhaling smoke. "I'm going through it."

Understanding where he was coming from, Moya ran a hand over his wavy hair and made her way to the truck. Her next mission was to see her mother and sisters.

"Sis?" Tron called out to her.

She stopped and looked back at him.

"Drive safe," he said.

Moya nodded and got in the truck.

At the hospital, she made her way upstairs to her sisters' room. Moya had a bad feeling she wasn't going to be able to hold in her tears. Her mother's call made it sound like her sisters were dead or something. That's how Moya knew it was gonna be bad.

The closer she got, the heavier her heart felt. The unknown was a muthafucka.

Five minutes later, she reached the room and paused at the door. Taking a deep breath, she opened it and walked inside—only to be hit with a sight that made her go off.

Roland, who had been sitting next to her mother, looked up and frowned.

"No the fuck you ain't!" Moya snapped, reaching for her pistol.

Without hesitation, she aimed at Roland and pulled the trigger, but he was already moving fast, ducking behind Toya's bed—which was empty now.

"Moya, no!" Naomi bellowed. "Stop!"

Moya aimed at the bed and sent a bullet through it, hoping it penetrated him.

"Don't hide, bitch nigga!"

Joya cowered under the covers, the whole room turning into a war zone.

"Bring your ass from behind—" Moya started before Toya stepped in front of her, her gaze stern.

"The hell you think you're doin', bitch?" Toya shouted.

"Bitch?" Moya glared at her.

"You trippin', sis! You need to leave—get outta here with that bullshit."

"You takin' up for that snake-ass nigga?"

"That nigga is our daddy."

Moya frowned.

"That nigga ain't my daddy!"

She caught a glimpse of Roland peeking out from behind the bed and aimed again, but before she could squeeze the trigger, Toya popped her in the mouth and dropped Moya to the floor.

Reaching a hand to her lips, Moya tasted blood.

"Moya, go!" their mother cried. "Please!"

Moya glared up at her twin. Toya glared right back.

"What you wanna do, Moya?"

"You wanna die too, bitch?" Moya said, standing and aiming the pistol straight at Toya's forehead.

Toya didn't budge.

"Stop!" Joya sobbed from the bed.

Naomi stepped in front of Toya, facing Moya with eyes hard as stone. There were no words needed at that moment.

"Fuck this shit . . . But I gotcha, twin."

Moya nodded grimly at Toya, then turned around and walked away. Before leaving, she tucked the pistol and made her exit.

Outside in the hallway, everybody was staring, but Moya kept her chin up and kept moving.

The line between her and Toya had been drawn.

She could die right along with Roland.

No exceptions.

Chapter 15

Zamon unlocked the door to his duplex apartment and led them inside. KeKe carried Malcolm over to the nearest sofa and laid him down gently. Next, she went to retrieve their bags while Zamon limped into his bedroom. He was tired. He was hurting. But most of all, he was disgruntled as fuck. And there was still a lot of work that needed to be done.

As Zamon plugged his phone in to charge, he dialed a number he desperately needed to call. Under different circumstances, he would've handled the business himself, but at that moment, he wasn't in any condition to do much. He needed help.

"What it do, Zee!" someone answered on the second ring.

"I need your help, Bebop," Zamon said. "I'm in a bind right now, and I don't trust nobody but you to help me."

"Where you at, bruh?"

"At my crib."

"Gimme about fifteen minutes. I'm there!"

After hanging up with his partner, Zamon called for KeKe, but she didn't respond. He eased up and limped his way back to the front. There he found KeKe curled up on the sofa, Malcolm asleep beside her.

With a groan, Zamon made the painful journey to grab a blanket and covered them both.

By the time Bebop showed up, Zamon was sitting outside on the stoop in front of the duplex, but Bebop hadn't come alone. He brought his dawg Lank with him. Both of these niggas were two peas in the same pod—brothers in every sense. Zamon knew he could count on them both to hold him down.

These were two big, stocky muthafuckas too, especially Lank, who was once an offensive lineman before going corrupt.

"What happened to you?" Bebop asked, eyeing the dark blotches of blood on Zamon's bandaged arm and leg.

"Got ate up by a dog."

"A dog?"

"One of them big Chow muthafuckas."

Bebop whistled and shook his head, well aware of how vicious those dogs could be.

"How the fuck that happen?"

Zamon didn't answer the question directly.

"Bebop."

"Yeah?"

"I got a body in the trunk."

"You got a what? Where?" Lank asked, his voice sharp.

"In the trunk, and I need to get rid of it—like ASAP!" The tone in Zamon's voice wasn't lost on either of them. The pain, the agony, the desperation—it was clear as day.

"You serious?" Bebop asked.

"Fuckin' right I am!"

Lank laid a heavy hand on Zamon's shoulder and gave it a reassuring squeeze.

"Don't sweat it, lil bruh. We gotcha. We know what to do. You just fall back and let us handle it."

"It's my mission," Zamon insisted. "I just need help."

"But you hurt, bruh," Bebop argued.

"I can't let that car be found."

Lank squeezed his shoulder again. "Chill, we got it."

Minutes later, after Zamon had emptied the car of all KeKe's personal belongings, he watched Bebop drive off with the body in the trunk. He felt conflicted about not being able to join them on the mission.

Zamon could only be grateful, though. He'd been through too much already.

***

Back inside the crib, Zamon locked the door and dragged himself over to the other sofa next to the one where KeKe lay sleeping. He sat there for a long time, watching them sleep, knowing how complicated things were about to get.

He had to help them for real now.

He owed them.

They needed him more than ever.

***

"Moya!" Naomi called out as she hurried after her daughter.

She caught up to Moya just as she reached the parking lot. Moya glanced back but kept walking.

"Moya, please hear me out!"

"What the fuck do you want, Mama?" Moya spun around, her face twisted with anger.

Naomi stopped short.

"Don't you dare speak to me that way, Moya. I'm your mother! I know you're upset about your father—"

"He ain't my father!"

At that moment, a police cruiser pulled up at the hospital entrance. Moya turned her back, shielding her face from the cops. As the car rolled to a stop at the curb, she spun back around and kept moving, her hand easing near her hip where her pistol rested—just in case.

Shit was already crucial.

Naomi followed her into the darkness of the parking lot.

Moya was just hopping into the truck when Naomi caught up to her.

"Will you at least let me say what I need to say before you take off?"

"I don't wanna talk about him."

"Your sister is dying, Moya."

Moya froze instantly. She stared at her mother, frustration pounding in her head.

"Who?"

"Joya."

"How?"

"She has AIDS, baby. She's dying up in that room right now."

Moya's heart sank.

"AIDS?" she whispered.

Naomi nodded.

Moya sat in stunned silence. Naomi went on to explain everything.

Moya roared in outrage, banging the steering wheel repeatedly. Naomi's motherly instincts kicked in, and she pulled Moya into her arms. They cried together.

"I can't go back in there," Moya sobbed. "I can't be in there with him, Mama. I'ma kill that nigga if I see him, Mama."

"You can't kill my husband."

"On everything I love, Mama," Moya hissed through clenched teeth. "I'ma murder his ass on sight. It's either him or me, and I love me over him any day!"

With that, Moya pushed her mother aside, shut the door, and sped off.

"Nooo!" she screamed as she drove, tears falling like rain.

She reached into her pocket, pulled out the half-ounce of Molly, popped two rocks, and snorted them.

"I wanna kill me a bitch!"

She stomped on the gas, running a red light, daring anybody to stop her.

She was ready for whatever.

***

The following morning, Desiree woke up to Monster bumping against the sofa, trying to pick a fight. He was hungry, and he wanted to be fed. Groggily, she got up and fed him. While doing so, Desiree decided to check on Heather. She found her still in the guest room, passed out cold, her mouth wide open and hanging halfway off the bed. Shaking her head, Desiree left her there and went to use the bathroom. A few moments later, the security system buzzed from downstairs. Good thing that Moya showed her how to use the security clearance machine, or whoever's out there would've stayed out there indefinitely. Desiree walked over to the machine, ready to press the button to see who it was, but Monster pushed her away, almost knocking her off balance. The dog let out a low threatening sound.

"What's your problem, ugly?' Desiree frowned.

Monster growled again. Then it clicked—what Moya had told her the night before: No one knew where she actually lived except for Heather, her twins, her mother, Ella Mae, and God. Oh, and Vonda—but Moya had only brought Vonda to the apartment building, not inside. And Roland? Nah, Desiree was certain he wouldn't be coming back there. So, who could it be?

"Who's at the door?" Heather asked sleepily, appearing in the foyer in her t-shirt and panties.

"I don't know," Desiree replied.

The buzzer sounded again, insistent this time. Heather reviewed the security footage on the screen mounted on the wall above the button. When she who it was, her breath got caught in her throat.

"It's my fiancé," she said, her voice barely audible, and then buzzed him through the gate.

Desiree frowned. "You know he can't come up here."

"I know," Heather admitted.

"So, what you gonna do?"

With a frustrated look on her face Heather hurried off to go put some clothes on.

"Don't open that door for no one!" she said firmly, glancing back at Desiree minutes later, as she headed for the front door.

"I won't," Desiree replied with a shrug.

As soon as the door shut behind her, Desiree scurried off into the kitchen with Monster right behind her. She pushed a stool up against the counter and climbed up to reach for the cabinet. She was looking for a specific bottle.

"Got it!" she said when she finally found the lemon pepper bottle.

Quickly, she unscrewed the cap and dumped a few of the OxyContin pills into her palm. She remembered where Moya had stashed them the night before. Until now, Heather had kept too close a watch for Desiree to get to them. Desiree was hurting, and Heather's aspirin pills weren't doing shit. She needed something stronger.

The house phone rang suddenly, startling her. Monster took off running from the kitchen, barking, and Desiree hurried after him to answer it.

"Hello?" Desiree said into the phone.

"Hi, Dez!" a very excited voice greeted her.

It was Josh. Desiree broke into a grin.

"Hey, Josh! What're you doing?" she asked.

True to her word, Moya had somehow gotten Desiree's number to Josh.

"Nothing. Mom is in a frantic!" Josh said.

"Why?"

"Because the cops came to my room looking for you. They thought you were hiding out here. How did you do it anyway, Dez?" he asked.

"I'll tell you when I see you again."

"You will?" Josh sounded thrilled at the prospect.

"Of course I will, Josh."

Just like always, they fell into an easy conversation, laughing and joking about everything. But in the back of her mind, Desiree couldn't shake the uneasy feeling. Where was Heather? Why hadn't she come back inside yet.

A sense of paranoia crept over her. Something wasn't right.

"I'll talk to you later," Desiree said to Josh, hanging up the phone abruptly. Then she rushed off to put some clothes on. She threw on a Prada outfit and some flats and tucked a pistol into her pants the way Moya had taught her.

Something was definitely wrong.

"Stay here, Monster!" she ordered the dog before opening the front door to go check on Heather.

She didn't even get far. Someone blocked her path.

Desiree gazed up at them, her throat tightening as she swallowed nervously.

And then all hell broke loose—hell like she'd never seen before.

Chapter 16

When Peanut woke up, he found himself in the county jail's holding tank, his back aching from laying on the hard bench for the past several hours. He couldn't believe his luck. His own mother had snitched on him and put him in jail over a nigga who didn't give a fuck about her in the first place. She went against her own son.

Overreacted my ass, Peanut thought, remembering his mother's words when she realized he was going to jail.

The bitch had actually told the police he killed Jon Boi, the same nigga the authorities had been looking for in connection with a string of killings. And where was his mother now while he sat in jail, probably facing the rest of his life behind bars? She was at home, getting torn up from the floor up. Emma should be ashamed of herself. Right now, Peanut wanted to kill her ass too.

"Perkins!" barked the guard standing at the door.

Peanut looked up.

"You're up. C'mon outta there, boy!" said the fat, bad-bodied white man with a cheek full of chewing tobacco.

Peanut got up, stretched his stiff limbs, popped his back, and headed for the door. He was finally given an orange jumpsuit and a bedroll to take with him to general population. The system was so backed up it wasn't even funny. So many people were getting locked up that they didn't have enough staff to process them fast enough. It took Peanut five and a half hours just to get a shot at laying down on something softer than a metal slab. Peanut was pissed the fuck off.

Good thing the cops didn't find the gun on him, or he'd really be fucked.

Minutes later, Peanut entered the general population pod and was directed to his cell by the officer keeping post inside the unit. For some reason, the pod was on lockdown, with everybody in their rooms. The transporting officer had already warned him he was headed to "gangland," meaning this particular pod was always locked down due to the constant stabbings and fights.

This wasn't Peanut's first rodeo, nor his second, so he was prepared for whatever. As he made his way to his room, Peanut recognized a few familiar faces. A couple of them called out greetings, but Peanut wasn't in the mood.

At his cell, the door buzzed open, and Peanut stepped inside with his belongings. His cellmate, an older cat Peanut recognized but couldn't quite place, sat up from the bottom bunk.

"How you doing, soldier?" the man asked.

"Sup." Peanut wasn't in the mood for conversation. All he wanted to do was lay down and figure out how the fuck he was getting out of there.

"What you in for?"

Peanut scowled darkly. "Look, old school, I ain't feelin' none of this shit right now. I don't feel like talkin'. All I wanna do is lay down and get some rest."

"I got no problem with that, son."

"And my name is Peanut! Not *soldier*, *son*, *homeboy*—none of that shit, a'ight?" Peanut snapped.

"Cool. I'm Brodrick. Get you some rest, Peanut."

Brodrick laid back down, but inside, he was waiting for the opportunity to check Peanut if he stepped wrong. Just like he planned to do to Desiree when he caught her little bad ass. He was going to put her down for good, just like he did her mother.

***

Ray Ray stepped out onto the front porch, followed by the rest of the crew—Spud, Bizkit, and Tron—all sharing a blunt to jump-start their day. The Youngins were still mourning their losses.

"She's still in there asleep," Ray Ray said.

Just before dawn, Moya had come into the house and gone straight to her room. Tron had been stretched across her bed, and she'd laid down beside him. No words were exchanged, just the sound of quiet sniffling as she cried herself to sleep. Tron had let her be before eventually getting up to give her some space.

"What do you think happened?" Bizkit asked.

"I don't know," Tron sighed. "I just hope Toya and Joya are alright."

"I wanna go see 'em," Spud said.

"Me too," Tron replied.

"But none of us know the way to the hospital, and besides, we can't leave Mo by herself." Bizkit passed the blunt to Ray Ray, who was already good and high. Now all he wanted was some food.

Across the street, the front door of a neighbor's house swung open, and Bobby walked out, heading toward his pickup truck. He glanced over at Naomi's house and spotted the Youngins on the porch. He paused. From where he stood, leaning against the post, Spud saw him approaching.

"Heads up!" Spud warned.

Ray Ray, Bizkit, and Tron snapped to attention, their eyes locked on Bobby as he approached with purpose.

"Morning," Bobby greeted them. "Y'all mind telling me what your business is here? I don't know y'all, and I need to know what's up."

"Who the fuck is you, nigga?" Spud shot back.

Bobby stepped up, chest out. "I'm Bobby Lucas."

That's when Tron stepped up right in his face.

"Well, check this out, *Bobby Brown*. You better take some of that air out your chest before I deflate that shit, playboy!"

"Don't threaten me, youngsta!" Bobby pointed a finger at Tron.

"Or what?" Ray Ray said, pulling his pistol.

The Youngins surrounded Bobby like a pack of wolves. Bobby knew he had to play it smart.

"Y'all chill," Bizkit intervened. "Not in Ms. Naomi's yard. It ain't going down like that."

"You know Naomi?" Bobby asked. "That's my woman."

"Your woman?"

"Yeah." Bobby nodded. "My woman."

The front door opened, and there stood Moya in a tank top and boxer shorts, her body on full display. She didn't take her looks seriously, but right now, anybody would swear she was a dime piece.

"Y'all leave my man Bobby alone," she said.

"So you know this nigga?" Bizkit asked.

Moya nodded. "He's good. Plus, y'all don't wanna see Mama's wrath if you fuck with him."

"You lucky," Spud muttered at Bobby. "I was about to bust your whole head."

Bobby shrugged.

"Sis," Tron said.

"What?" Moya snapped.

"Put on some clothes. We're hungry, and you need to take care of your business."

"Okay, big little brother." She shut the door behind her, leaving Bobby to fend for himself.

"You can leave now, Bobby Brown!" Ray Ray smirked, his pistol still in hand.

"A'ight then," Bobby backed away cautiously. "Y'all be cool."

The Youngins didn't have any more words for him. They wanted food. They wanted blood.

***

KeKe stepped out of the bathroom to the sounds of choking sobs coming from the bedroom. She eased over towards the partially opened door and peered inside. Rolling around on the floor beside the bed was Zamon, crying so hard his whole body was shaking. This was the last thing she expected to see.

KeKe was moved by the sight. *Something very bad must have happened to him*, she thought as she watched Zamon sob like a baby. Although his injuries were bad, KeKe doubted they alone would have him in a state like this. His emotions ran deeper than rap—something else was burning his heart, breaking him down like that.

Joya. KeKe knew it had to be her. Given the fact that she was in the hospital, it only made sense. Then there was the cell phone clutched in Zamon's hand. In her heart of hearts, she knew it was Joya because only a woman could have a man crying his heart out like he was dying inside.

"Go to him." her heart told her. *"He needs you!"*

And that's exactly what she did, bursting into the room and falling to her knees next to him.

Then she pulled him into her arms, and he clung to her for dear life. Zamon buried face into her chest and sobbed hard, so hard it made her own eyes water.

"What's wrong, Zamon?" she whispered to him.

"She killed me!" he choked out.

"Killed you? She *killed* you how?"

He cried continuously.

"Talk to me, honey. That's what I'm here for," she said in a soothing voice. "I'm here for you, Zamon." KeKe rocked him in her arms like she'd done Malcolm so many times over the years.

After he'd cried himself empty and calmed down enough to speak, his words hit KeKe's heart like nothing ever had before.

"I'm dying of AIDS, KeKe," he said.

"What!" She froze, looking down at him in shock.

Zamon nodded slowly.

"You have AIDS?" she asked, disbelief etched across her face.

"That was Joya on the phone," he said.

Zamon went into detail about their conversation—how he had snapped on her, threatened to kill her for what she did to him. Then, before he knew it, broke down and cried. KeKe held him even tighter.

"I can't live like this," Zamon whispered. "My life is over. I can't believe she did this shit to me," he cried.

I can't either, thought KeKe.

"You gotta stay strong, Zamon," she said. "For me and Malcolm. We need you more than anything. I'm not going nowhere. We're still in this shit together. Okay?"

"But I'm dying," he muttered.

"We all eventually die," she kissed the side of his head gently. "As long as we have breath in our bodies, we must give our best. We only have one life to live, Zamon. And you got me now. So get your shit together, because we got a lot more life to live for."

Zamon looked up at her, searching her face. "You mean that?"

"I mean it with my life," she said.

What more could a nigga really ask for?

Chapter 17

His name was Greg Reynolds, and he lived right across the hall from Moya. He and Moya knew each other well. She was interested in his passion for painting. It was a year ago when she first moved in, and they bumped into each other in the hallway while Greg was carrying one of his large framed paintings out to display at a local gallery.

"What's that?" Moya had asked, lifting up a corner of the cloth draped over the frame.

"It's a painting of mine," he said.

"You paint?" she replied.

"Most certainly." Greg revealed his art for her to see. "I'm going to auction it off tonight at a big convention downtown at the Art Center. If it sells, this will be my fourth piece."

"How much is it worth?"

"The starting bid is $2,100," he told her confidently.

"That much for a variety of colors blended together to make something I can't even tell what it is?"

"It's more than just a variety of colors."

"I want it!" Moya snatched the painting from him and started digging in her pocket for the money.

Greg thought she was bullshitting, but not only did she purchase that one painting, she ended up buying two more after he took her into his condo-turned-studio to show off the rest of his collection. From that moment on, they had become tight. Moya was a huge supporter of his work, so Greg felt it was only right to return the favor by intervening in a business he knew nothing about. But he knew Heather.

The moment Greg entered the building and saw Heather and Avery surrounded by three angry-looking dudes and an even meaner-looking woman, he knew something serious was going down. He bypassed the altercation after noticing two of the men were strapped, but when he overheard them violently demanding the little girl's whereabouts from Heather, he knew he had to do something.

Moya would want me to save the girl.

Greg hurried upstairs, and just as he turned toward the apartment door, it opened. When he saw the little girl standing there, he snapped into action.

"There's trouble coming your way, Desiree!" he said.

"Huh? Do I know you?"

"You gotta get out of here now," he said, grabbing her arm.

"Lemme go!" Desiree snatched away from him.

"I need to get you to safety!"

That's when Monster struck.

The massive dog charged into Greg so hard the force knocked him down, with Desiree landing right on top of him. Then, straight savagery happened—Monster went for the man's throat and ripped it open. Blood gushed out like a busted waterbed.

"Monster, no!" Desiree screamed frantically. "Stop!"

But Monster wasn't hearing her. He was in kill mode, and Greg didn't stand a chance.

In the process, the elevator doors slid open, and out stepped Wanda—the girl's darkest nightmare, her evil gaze shining like a death omen. Desiree looked up, saw Wanda, and panicked like a frightened kitten.

Then Desiree reached for the pistol.

Wanda froze when she saw the girl with the gun. Something in her told her to duck, but she didn't think Desiree had the heart to pull the trigger.

Boom!

***

Toya was talking to her father over bagels and hot chocolate when something inside her stirred—her gut instincts kicking in strong. Mid-sentence, she bolted to her feet.

"What is it?" Roland asked.

Without a word, Toya rushed to the bathroom where Joya had locked herself in. Their mother had given Joya the phone earlier to talk to Zamon in private, something she had been pushing for all night. Despite her wired jaw, Joya had insisted she could still get her point across.

"Baby girl, what's wrong?" Roland set his cup down and got up.

Toya stood outside the bathroom door. "Twin?" she knocked. "You alright in there?"

No answer.

"Joya, say something. You okay?"

"Maybe she just wants to be alone right now," Roland suggested.

Toya shot him a grave look. "She's been in there too long." She knocked harder. "Come to the door, Joya. I just wanna make sure you're okay."

Still no response. Roland tried the door—locked. Pressing her ear against it, Toya heard nothing.

"Joya?" she whispered.

"We gotta get that door open," said Roland, his face mirroring Toya's fear.

That was all the encouragement she needed. She stepped back and kicked the door twice, breaking it open.

"Oh my God! Twin!" Toya screamed in horror.

Joya was sprawled out on the bathroom floor, her wrists slit. The shattered phone lay nearby, its jagged pieces covered in blood. Roland sprinted to get help while Toya cradled her twin, sobbing uncontrollably.

"Why?" she wailed. "Wake up! Please, Joya, wake up!"

By the time Roland returned with the medical staff, it was too late. Joya was gone.

***

Meanwhile, the bullet struck Wanda dead center in her stomach, sending her stumbling back into the elevator. She hollered, and Monster was on her in an instant. His bloody mouth snarled as he tore into her face.

Desiree watched in horror from the floor. Wanda's screams were enough to shake even the devil himself.

"That's enough, Monster!" Desiree pleaded, stomping her feet stubbornly. "C'mon, let her go!"

Monster wasn't listening.

Then the emergency exit door burst open, and two men stormed into the hallway. Desiree recognized Wanda's brother and cousin.

Tim saw his sister's mangled body and pulled his gun, charging toward the elevator. Monster looked up, eyes locking onto him, then lunged.

Boom! A shot to the head put Monster down.

Desiree screamed and fired back, putting a bullet through Tim's back.

Heather burst through the door just as Desiree aimed at the second guy.

"Dez!" Heather shoved him aside and ran to the girl.

Desiree was trembling, fear radiating through her body.

"You left me," she whimpered.

Doug, Wanda's cousin, snapped out of his shock when Heather suddenly appeared in the hallway. He reached for his piece, but Desiree had already lifted the gun, aiming it right at him.

"Whoa!" Avery skidded to a stop behind Doug, his hands flying up in surrender, looking frantic and scared out of his damn mind.

Heather's eyes widened in disbelief when she saw Avery. She hadn't realized he'd brought Doug with him earlier, not until now. But none of that mattered anymore. She snatched the pistol from Desiree's trembling hands and turned it on Avery.

Boom!

She shot him point-blank in the head, sending him crashing to the floor like a sack of bricks.

"Marry that, muthafucker!" Heather sneered, her voice dripping with venom.

Desiree gasped, frozen in place, staring at Avery's lifeless body.

Doug took a hesitant step back, his eyes darting toward Tim's bloodied corpse lying nearby, and he knew his ass was next.

"Both of y'all, lay down!" Heather barked, her aim shifting between Doug and the other man who'd crept up behind Avery unnoticed until now—probably one of Wanda's other lackeys.

Without hesitation, they obeyed, faces pressed against the cold-ass floor.

"Suckas," Heather muttered before putting two cold shots in the back of their heads, execution style.

Desiree stared wide-eyed. Heather was a gangster—hell, it ran in the family.

Chapter 18

During that same moment, Moya and her Youngins were fed and chilling with some of her people. She had made her rounds and was still pulling up on the set, making her presence known. Right now, they were over on the east side, kicking it with her cousins, Rel and Kita. Other than Daisy and her Aunt Cookie, these two were the only relatives Moya really fucked with on her mother's side. The rest of them was flawed—except for her grandmother, Mama Lillie. Moya and her sisters were crazy over her before she passed five years ago. Mama Lillie was deep in her seventies when she let a punk-ass heart attack take her out.

Where Ella Mae was the true gangster, Mama Lillie was the flower—the sweetest slice of pie you'll ever taste. She was the best.

Having been around long enough to command respect, the Youngins finally seemed more relaxed. They were vibing with Moya's people naturally, blowing on good weed and cooling. But of course, there were always niggas lurking in the cut, watching with silent envy. Niggas love to hate when they see other niggas doing better. The Youngins weren't sleep, though. They made sure their straps were visible, letting them niggas know that shit wasn't sweet.

"You heard about PeeWee?" asked Rel, a tall, brown-skinned nigga rocking designer braids and dripping in dope-boy fresh attire. This was the same nigga Moya used to run capers with back in the day.

"What about him?" Moya wasn't too fond of PeeWee—thought he was phony as hell. A coward with money.

Rel told her about the murder, but she was already hip to what went down. Moya listened intently, curious to see how far the story had stretched.

"They say some nigga named Zamon did the shit," Kita chimed in.

Now, Kita was one of them jet-black ghetto bitches who didn't give a fuck. She was doing her thing boosting and running credit card scams, raking in major cash.

"Zamon?" Ray Ray looked up.

"Yeah. Some out-of-town nigga," Kita said.

Tron and Spud exchanged quiet looks. Moya shrugged nonchalantly, not giving away the fact she knew exactly who Zamon was. She had already spoken to Daisy, who gave her the full scoop on what went down with him and her twin. But to hear that a nigga named Zamon was being blamed for PeeWee's murder? That shit hit different. There was only one Zamon she knew—and yeah, he was from out of town.

"Any idea where this nigga at?" Moya asked.

"I really don't give a fuck," Rel replied. "I don't fuck wit' that chump anyway. The nigga shoulda murked all them pussy niggas round there!"

Niggas knew better than to test Rel's gangster. Moya glanced over at Kita, who just shrugged.

"You know I don't give a fuck, cuz," she said, flashing a grin at Bizkit, letting the Youngin know she was feeling him. Kita thought the little nigga was sexy and was plotting to throw that good pussy on him.

"Look who's pullin' up in the trap," Rel nodded up the street at the approaching whip.

Moya's heart flipped.

All eyes were on the all-black and silver Audi R8 creeping up behind the Yukon Denali. When Dexter Carter stepped out looking like a homemade German chocolate cake, Moya sighed, her pussy instantly wet. This was *her nigga.* The only one who had the key to that sweet spot between her legs. The only one who ever really fucked her right—and she was ready for him to bust it wide open.

***

Zamon was hurting bad inside. He was scared, but the drive to live for something beyond his own selfish desires was fuel enough to keep him going. KeKe was right—he still had life left to live.

"Why not live it to the fullest?" he mumbled to himself as he entered Joya's apartment with his spare key.

He was about to hit her up good.

Zamon knew Joya cherished her expensive clothes and her secret stash. The clothes didn't matter to him. It was the safe in her bedroom that he was after.

In her closet, he yanked down her coats and dresses, gritting through the pain in his arm. There it was—right at the back. He knew the code; it was always the same damn thing—her birth date. Typical.

The safe clicked open, and what he saw inside made his mouth drop.

Stacks on stacks of cash. Some bound in rubber bands, others neatly wrapped in bank straps. Nearly $300,000 sat right in front of him, plus precious jewels and a thick-ass file folder.

Curiosity got the best of him. Flipping through the folder, Zamon realized Joya had been keeping receipts—evidence on all her victims. Photos, documents, notes, even some damn CDs.

"Damn, this bitch wasn't playing," he muttered.

Without wasting time, Zamon packed the cash and evidence into one of Joya's rolling suitcases and dragged it to the door.

***

At Cookie's Bakery, Naomi was sitting across from Bobby, doing her best not to break his heart completely. She needed this moment with him—this closure.

Bobby, though? He wasn't taking it well.

"I mean, it is what it is, Bobby. I'm sorry," Naomi said, her voice low but firm.

Bobby frowned. "You never stopped loving him."

"You knew that already, Bobby."

"Every time we made love, it was Roland you was thinking about, not me," he said, his voice breaking.

"That's not true, Bobby. I love you. I always—"

Bobby shook his head, standing up abruptly. "I'll be damned if I let that nigga come back and take you away from me."

Naomi saw something dark and ominous in his eyes.

"What do you mean?"

"If I can't have you, Naomi, no one will."

"Bobby, don't do this," she pleaded.

Bobby sneered. "It's already done."

With that, he stormed out the door, kicking it on his way out.

"You better stop kicking my shit!" Cookie yelled out after Bobby from behind the counter.

As soon as the door shut, it swung right back open, and Elijah walked in looking annoyed. He glanced back at the door, his frown deepening. He must have just bumped into Bobby on his way in, which could only explain why he looked that way. Naomi was surprised to see him. Elijah locked eyes with Toya's mother and headed straight for her.

"Hello, Elijah!" Cookie greeted stubbornly as he walked past her without speaking.

"What are you doing here?" Naomi asked.

"What did you do to your boyfriend?" he shot back.

In the last twelve months since Elijah and Toya had been together, they had never visited Jacksonville as a couple. Toya hadn't been there in nearly a year, while Elijah had only visited a few times himself. Some of his good friends lived in Jacksonville, and Cookie's Bakery was one of his favorite spots ever since Toya insisted he check it out. He and Naomi only knew each other through social media and only meeting her twice in person. Their acquaintance was yet to be made tight.

"I need to see my girl," he said, settling into the same seat Bobby had just vacated. "I took the day off to come check up on Toya. I received a text that she was in the hospital, so I came through."

"This is a bad time for us, Elijah," Naomi said, rubbing her temple.

"That's why I'm here," he replied.

The phone rang from the front counter.

Elijah leaned forward, his eyes glistening with concern. "How is she really?"

Naomi released a heavy sigh, but before she could respond, a piercing scream erupted. Her head snapped towards the counter, where her sister stood clutching the phone to her ear, her face pale.

Then Cookie stared at Naomi and let out at another heart-wrenching wail that sent chills up her spine.

Naomi shot to her feet instantly.

"What's wrong, Cookie?"

"She's gone, sis!" Cookie told Naomi, sobbing like she had just lost her best friend.

"Who's gone?" Naomi hurried over, heart pounding.

"Joya!" Cookie cried out. "She killed herself! She's dead!"

Naomi's knees buckled beneath her. That was the last thing she remembered before everything went black.

Chapter 19

Moya growled as she bounced up and down on that dick like she was riding a bronco bull. Dex had her all filled up, and it hurt so damn good. She was riding that dick sideways and all, making sure she watched how her ass was throwing it back at him.

Then she climbed off Dex and looked down at him with a hungry look in her eyes.

"What's that, baby?" he groaned.

"I'm about to break that dick off in me," she said.

She stalked around the bedroom and pressed herself against the wall by the door, looking back at him.

"Come beat this pussy from the back, nigga," Moya commanded.

Dex got up, stepping closer to her sexy, naked body, her ass tooted up in the air.

"You miss this dick, don't you?" he murmured, sliding up behind her.

"Nigga, just fuck me and stop talkin'!"

"You got it," Dex smirked.

He slid inside her from the back, grabbing her waist and digging off in that pussy like he was mining for gold.

Moya's phone started ringing.

"Ahh! Ah! Ah! Damn, you slangin' that big dick!" Moya moaned. "Get all up in that shit, nigga!" She pushed back against him.

"I'm in it!" he grunted.

"Get it!" she moaned, ignoring the phone.

But as he pounded her, Moya suddenly felt a sense of alarm creep over her. She froze, staring at the wall, then shoved Dex the fuck off her. Panic flooded her face as she scrambled for her clothes.

"What's up, Moya?" Dex stared at her, confused.

"I gotta go!"

"Go where?"

Dex looked down at his tool, which was softening by the second. Moya didn't answer as she pulled on her Dickies and laced up her Air Jordans. Her pussy was throbbing, but not as much as her heart was. Something was wrong with one of her twins—she could feel it in her soul.

Dex watched helplessly. He couldn't stop her. He would never stop her from doing what she wanted—not even if he tried.

"*But damn*," Dex thought to himself.

That pussy was fire. The best he ever had.

"I'll hit you up later," Moya called back.

And then she was gone.

***

Outside, her Youngins were standing guard like mercenaries. They had followed behind Dex's car all the way to his house, making sure Moya was safe. Now, they were back on the move once more, the urgency clear as Moya dashed out of the house like a frightened cat.

"What's the deal?" Ray Ray asked. "What's up?"

"That nigga cross you, sis?" Tron reached for the Mac-11 in the backseat, ready to pop off.

"It's something else," Bizkit said, watching Moya climb behind the wheel with a frantic look on her face.

All of them piled into the truck just before Moya peeled off like a bat out of hell.

"Something's wrong," Moya said, her voice shaking. "I can feel it! I can feel something's wrong wit' one of my twins."

Her phone rang again, and Bizkit snatched it up.

"It's your cousin Daisy," he said, checking the screen.

"Answer it."

He picked up the call.

"Hello?"

Moments later, Bizkit dropped his head dejectedly, his face dark with sorrow.

Moya's eyes burned with desperation. "What's she sayin'?"

Bizkit swallowed hard. "It's Joya," he muttered.

Moya's heart squeezed with fear. "What about Joya? What's wrong wit' my twin?"

"She's dead," he said flatly.

"What!"

The entire truck fell silent.

Moya felt her whole world come crashing down. Her twin was dead.

***

In the kitchen, Ella Mae was frying gizzards when the front door opened and shut. Heather walked in with Desiree in tow, and the old woman immediately opened her arms. Desiree stepped into her embrace, her face sullen. She was high, still floating from the pill she'd popped earlier. The confrontation with Greg had aggravated her injured ribs, and Ella Mae quickly noticed the blood on the girl's clothes.

"What happened?" Ella Mae asked, turning off the stove and setting the frying pan aside.

"Avery is dead, Mama," Heather said.

"Dead?"

"I killed him."

Ella Mae released Desiree's hand in shock. "What do you mean you killed him? Kill him how? Why?" She pulled out a chair and sat down heavily.

Heather sat down too. "I had to, Mama."

"He set us up," Desiree added.

For the next ten minutes, they recounted everything that had happened at the condo. Ella Mae sighed, thinking of how upset Moya would be about Monster's death.

"That man let them bitch him up, Mama," Heather said angrily. "Wanda came after Dez, and they brought guns with them."

"And this other man—who was he?" Ella Mae asked.

"Greg, from across the hall."

"And he died trying to save the girl," the old woman said sadly. "I told Moya that damn dog was gonna kill somebody."

"And it sure did."

Desiree, without asking, opened the fridge, looking for something to drink. The Oxy had her mouth dry as hell.

"So there were no witnesses?" Ella Mae asked.

"Not that I know of," Heather replied.

Ella Mae fixed Desiree another cup of Pepsi, shaking her head. "And once they realize who Wanda is, they'll come lookin' for the girl."

"I know."

"So what're we gonna do?"

Desiree raised her hand. "I know," she said.

Both women turned to look at her.

"I can go stay with Naomi," she suggested. "I wanna go to Jacksonville with everybody else."

The phone rang. It was Roland.

Bad news was spreading fast, just like social media.

***

Noah and his two comrades had finally landed from the skies onto Florida's soil, and they hadn't come to play either. As soon as they made it through safely, Noah called his father's phone.

No answer.

Noah tried a second time—still no answer.

Where the fuck was his father, and why wasn't he picking up? Was he okay? He *better* be okay, or there was going to be hell to pay.

To speed matters up, Noah had his partner, Flex, lease on of the airline's rental vehicles. Now they had wheels and was moving by GPS, headed directly to FAMU's college campus. Noah had heard about the all-black college and wanted to see for himself, but pleasure wasn't on the itinerary. They were there for one thing only—information.

As they rode through the big city, Noah repeatedly tried Roland's phone, to no avail. That shit was beginning to piss him the fuck off. Meanwhile, in the backseat, Sonny—the deadliest one out of the three—scrolled through his phone, reading the latest news that was going on in the city.

"We've entered a fuckin' warzone," said Flex.

"And with no guns or nothing," Noah added.

That's the major issue Sonny was stressing the entire flight over. He was a shooter straight out the Bricks City territory, where all he knew was that goon shit. Getting shot four times—on two different occasions—was all the reason he needed to tote that steel.

Flex too was on his thug shit, but he wasn't Sonny. He and Noah had been cronies since the sandbox, and while he had no problem pulling that trigger too, he just wasn't a natural-born killer. But for Noah? He would kill without hesitation.

"I think I found something," Sonny muttered, still glued to his phone.

"What is it?" Noah asked.

"This Moya chick—I found some shit on her. She got twin sistas—"

"She's one of the twins, Sonny."

"Nah, they triplets, yeah, I got that!" Sonny said, still scrolling. "But check this out—she got a Facebook account, and this shit is loaded. I'm seein' all kinds of shit, bro. She owns a car detail shop, a daycare, and even a fuckin' hair salon. This chick is into some real bread! And peep this— she got flicks with some big-money niggas too. She really on her boss shit."

"That's who we need to be contacting then," Noah said as they pulled up onto the college campus.

The scene in front of them was wild—females everywhere. Bitches galore, and not one of them was ugly yet.

"This is crazy," Flex said, wide-eyed.

"Damn," was all he could manage as they rolled through the set like they were in a parade.

But Sonny wasn't paying attention to the bitches. His mind was stuck on one bitch—Moya. She had him captivated, like she was actually talking to him through the screen. She was *that* bitch for real, and he couldn't wait to finally meet her in person.

If only he knew.

Moya was trouble—more trouble than he could ever imagine.

Chapter 20

The funeral for Joya Scott was packed with family, friends, and even a few enemies whom she had done dirty throughout the years. But through it all, she was loved by many, and her death left them devastated. The church could barely fit everybody in the room. Naomi thought it would be best to have the funeral back home in Jacksonville after the mourning wake service they held for Joya in Tallahassee. Even those who have come to pay their respects there was even back here today.

Joya had died young and beautiful, and many hearts were broken because of it. It was one of the saddest moments ever, with everyone staring at her casket sitting before the altar. Joya had touched a lot of people's lives—even Roland's, who sat up front, but as far away from Moya as possible. Although he hadn't been around to watch Joya grow up to her full potential, he had come back just in time to meet her in that glory. He had returned right on time to see her smile before she died. Even through her pain, she did it—and what a beautiful smile that was. Roland would never forget that smile.

Across from him, at the front of the church, sat Naomi flanked by Moya and Toya, and even Tron was there too, standing strong for them. While everybody else was dressed in suits and dresses, Moya rocked an all-black Gucci outfit with matching black Air Forces to keep it street. And, of course, she was strapped. All her Youngins were.

While the reverend stood in the pulpit preaching the gospel, Toya held her mother, offering what little comfort she could. Naomi was torn to pieces. She hadn't stopped crying yet since Joya's death.

Moya, too, was forcing herself not to cry. Too many people were watching. Her gold-framed Ray-Ban sunglasses hid her weary eyes.

"It's going to be okay, Mama," Toya whispered, doing her best to soothe her mother. "She's in a better place now. Joya isn't suffering anymore." Toya knew she had to be strong for her family now.

Naomi cried softly into her daughter's shoulder.

"What am I going to do without my baby?" she mourned.

"She's still with us in heart, Mama. Now stop crying," Toya said, wiping Naomi's face. "You're messing up your makeup."

Moya shook her head, reached into her pocket, and pulled out a blunt. Right there in the church, she lit it up. She couldn't take it no more. She needed something to ease her nerves.

When the weed smoke floated into the air, everybody looked in Moya's direction. But behind those dark shades, Moya kept looking straight ahead, puffing away like she didn't have a care in the world. She didn't give a fuck about nothing.

"Put that mess out!" Toya turned to her and said.

Moya hit the blunt again, and exhaled a train weed smoke into the air. The reverend gazed out into the congregation at Moya, but he didn't dare rebuke her. All he did was amplify his voice so that the people would focus on all their attention on him. No one said shit. They weren't stupid.

"Moya," Ella Mae's sharp voice cut through the crowd from across the aisle. "Put it out or get out!"

And that's exactly what Moya decided to do, and rose up to her feet. She took another puff from her blunt and blew smoke in the air. She then approached Joya's casket, staring down at her twin one last time.

"I love you, Twin. I'll see you again. Till then, watch over me as I do my thing down here."

Moya leaned down, kissed Joya's cheek, put the blunt back in her mouth, and walked out.

At once, a total of twenty-seven Youngins stood up throughout the church. Moving in harmony, they followed their queen outside like the loyal soldiers they were. Their presence was felt. Heavy.

Yeah, Moya had built another team of young killaz, and they were just as ruthless as her.

It was time to change the game.

Shit just got critical.

When it rains, it pours.

Lock Down Publications and Ca$h Presents Assisted Publishing Packages

Due to an increase in the price of services we have increased our prices. The prices below reflect the price increase as of 11/1/24.

BASIC PACKAGE	UPGRADED PACKAGE
$699	**$1000**
Editing	Typing
Cover Design	Editing
Formatting	Cover Design
	Formatting
	Upload eBooks to Amazon
	Upload Paperback to Amazon
ADVANCE PACKAGE	**LDP SUPREME PACKAGE**
$1,400	**$1,700**
Typing	Typing
Editing (line editing/content)	Editing (line editing/content)
Cover Design	Cover Design
Formatting	Formatting
Copyright Registration	Copyright Registration
Proofreading	Proofreading
Upload eBooks to Amazon	Set up Amazon Account
Upload Paperback to Amazon	Upload eBooks to Amazon
	Upload Paperback to Amazon
	Advertise on LDP's Amazon and Facebook Page

NEW RELEASES

BLOODLINE OF A SAVAGE 1-3
THESE VICIOUS STREETS 1-3
RELENTLESS GOON 1-3
BY PRINCE A. TAUHID

THE BUTTERFLY MAFIA 1-3
BY FUMIYA PAYNE

A THUG'S STREET PRINCESS 1&2
BY MEESHA

CITY OF SMOKE 3
BY MOLOTTI

GET IT IN SLUGS 1 &2
BY B. STALL

STANDING ON HER BUSINESS 1&2
BY DG SANTANA

STEPPERS 1,2&3
THE REAL BADDIES OF CHI-RAQ
BY KING RIO

THE LANE 1&2
BY KEN-KEN SPENCE

THUG OF SPADES 1&2
LOVE IN THE TRENCHES 2
CORNER BOYS
BY COREY ROBINSON

TIL DEATH 3
BY ARYANNA

THE BIRTH OF A GANGSTER 4
BY DELMONT PLAYER

PRODUCT OF THE STREETS 1-3
BY DEMOND "MONEY" ANDERSON

NO TIME FOR ERROR
BY KEESE

MONEY HUNGRY DEMONS 1-2
BY TRANAY ADAMS

HUB CITY MENACE 1-3
BY J. WHITE

A THUGGISH PASSION 1&2
LAND OF DA HOOLIGANZ 1-4
KILLAZ ON STANDBY 1&2
BY IRA B.

FO'EVA ROLLIN 1&2
BY ASSA RAYMOND BAKER

THE LEVEL UP 1&3
BY LUXURY KING

Coming Soon from Lock Down Publications/Ca$h Presents

IF YOU CROSS ME ONCE 6
ANGEL V
By Anthony Fields

A THUGS STREET PRINCESS 3
By Meesha

CORNER BOYS 2
By Corey Robinson

THA TAKEOVER
By Keith Chandler

BETRAYAL OF A G 2
By Ray Vinci

SAVAGE FAMILY EMPIRE 1&2
SOULLESS GOON 1,2&3
THE DIRTY SIDE OF MONEY 1,2&3
By Prince

FOR MY ENEMY'S SAKE
AMBITIONS OF A SLIDER
FRESH OFF DA PORCH
By IRA B.

THE TRUCKLOAD 1-4
TIPPIN' THE SCALES 1-3
BAD BITCHES WIT GUNZ 3
PROBLEM SOLVED 2
By Christopher "Diesel" Hornezes

Available Now

RESTRAINING ORDER 1 & 2
By **CA$H & Coffee**

LOVE KNOWS NO BOUNDARIES 1-3
By **Coffee**

RAISED AS A GOON I, II, III & IV
BRED BY THE SLUMS I, II, III
BLAST FOR ME I & II
ROTTEN TO THE CORE I II III
A BRONX TALE I, II, III
DUFFLE BAG CARTEL I II III IV V VI
HEARTLESS GOON I II III IV V
A SAVAGE DOPEBOY I II
DRUG LORDS I II III
CUTTHROAT MAFIA I II
KING OF THE TRENCHES
By **Ghost**

LAY IT DOWN I & II
LAST OF A DYING BREED I II
BLOOD STAINS OF A SHOTTA I & II III
By **Jamaica**

LOYAL TO THE GAME I II III
LIFE OF SIN I, II III
By **TJ & Jelissa**

IF LOVING HIM IS WRONG…I & II
LOVE ME EVEN WHEN IT HURTS I II III
By **Jelissa**

PUSH IT TO THE LIMIT
By **Bre' Hayes**

BLOODY COMMAS I & II
SKI MASK CARTEL I, II & III
KING OF NEW YORK I II, III IV V
RISE TO POWER I II III
COKE KINGS I II III IV V
BORN HEARTLESS I II III IV
KING OF THE TRAP I II
By **T.J. Edwards**

WHEN THE STREETS CLAP BACK I & II III
THE HEART OF A SAVAGE I II III IV
MONEY MAFIA I II
LOYAL TO THE SOIL I II III
By **Jibril Williams**

A DISTINGUISHED THUG STOLE MY HEART I II & III
LOVE SHOULDN'T HURT I II III IV
RENEGADE BOYS 1-4
PAID IN KARMA 1-3
SAVAGE STORMS 1-3
AN UNFORESEEN LOVE 1-3

BABY, I'M WINTERTIME COLD 1-3
A THUG'S STREET PRINCESS 1&2
By **Meesha**

A GANGSTER'S CODE 1-3
A GANGSTER'S SYN 1-3
THE SAVAGE LIFE 1-3
CHAINED TO THE STREETS 1-3
BLOOD ON THE MONEY 1-3
A GANGSTA'S PAIN 1-3
BEAUTIFUL LIES AND UGLY TRUTHS
CHURCH IN THESE STREETS
By **J-Blunt**

CUM FOR ME 1-8
An LDP Erotica Collaboration

BLOOD OF A BOSS 1-5
SHADOWS OF THE GAME
TRAP BASTARD
By **Askari**

THE STREETS BLEED MURDER 1-3
THE HEART OF A GANGSTA 1-3
By **Jerry Jackson**

WHEN A GOOD GIRL GOES BAD
By **Adrienne**

THE COST OF LOYALTY 1-3
By **Kweli**

BRIDE OF A HUSTLA 1-3
THE FETTI GIRLS 1-3
CORRUPTED BY A GANGSTA 1-4
BLINDED BY HIS LOVE
THE PRICE YOU PAY FOR LOVE 1-3
DOPE GIRL MAGIC 1-3

By **Destiny Skai**

A KINGPIN'S AMBITION
A KINGPIN'S AMBITION II
I MURDER FOR THE DOUGH
By **Ambitious**

TRUE SAVAGE 1-7
DOPE BOY MAGIC 1-3
MIDNIGHT CARTEL 1-3
CITY OF KINGZ 1&2
NIGHTMARE ON SILENT AVE
THE PLUG OF LIL MEXICO 1&2
CLASSIC CITY
By **Chris Green**

A GANGSTER'S REVENGE 1-4
THE BOSS MAN'S DAUGHTERS 1-5
A SAVAGE LOVE 1&2
BAE BELONGS TO ME 1&2
A HUSTLER'S DECEIT 1-3
WHAT BAD BITCHES DO 1-3
SOUL OF A MONSTER 1-3
KILL ZONE
A DOPE BOY'S QUEEN 1-3
TIL DEATH 1-3
IMMA DIE BOUT MINE 1-6
DYING FOR LIKES
By **Aryanna**

A DOPEBOY'S PRAYER
By **Eddie "Wolf" Lee**

THE KING CARTEL 1-3
By **Frank Gresham**

THESE NIGGAS AIN'T LOYAL 1-3

KILLAZ ON STANDBY 2 | IRA B

By **Nikki Tee**

GANGSTA SHYT 1-3
By **CATO**

THE ULTIMATE BETRAYAL
By **Phoenix**

BOSS'N UP 1-3
By **Royal Nicole**

I LOVE YOU TO DEATH
By **Destiny J**

I RIDE FOR MY HITTA
I STILL RIDE FOR MY HITTA
By **Misty Holt**

LOVE & CHASIN' PAPER
By **Qay Crockett**

TO DIE IN VAIN
SINS OF A HUSTLA
By **ASAD**

BROOKLYN HUSTLAZ
By **Boogsy Morina**

BROOKLYN ON LOCK 1 & 2
By **Sonovia**

GANGSTA CITY
By **Teddy Duke**

A DRUG KING AND HIS DIAMOND 1-3
A DOPEMAN'S RICHES
HER MAN, MINE'S TOO 1&2
CASH MONEY HO'S
THE WIFEY I USED TO BE 1&2

PRETTY GIRLS DO NASTY THINGS
By **Nicole Goosby**

LIPSTICK KILLAH 1-3
CRIME OF PASSION 1-3
FRIEND OR FOE 1-3
By **Mimi**

TRAPHOUSE KING 1-3
KINGPIN KILLAZ 1-3
STREET KINGS 1&2
PAID IN BLOOD 1&2
CARTEL KILLAZ 1-3
DOPE GODS 1&2
By **Hood Rich**

THE STREETS ARE CALLING
By **Duquie Wilson**

STEADY MOBBN' 1-3
THE STREETS STAINED MY SOUL 1-3
By **Marcellus Allen**

WHO SHOT YA 1-3
SON OF A DOPE FIEND 1-4
HEAVEN GOT A GHETTO 1&2
SKI MASK MONEY 1&2
By **Renta**

GORILLAZ IN THE BAY 1-4
TEARS OF A GANGSTA 1/&2
3X KRAZY 1&2
STRAIGHT BEAST MODE 1&2
By **DE'KARI**

TRIGGADALE 1-3
MURDA WAS THE CASE 1-3
By **Elijah R. Freeman**

SLAUGHTER GANG 1-3
RUTHLESS HEART 1-3
By **Willie Slaughter**

GOD BLESS THE TRAPPERS 1-3
THESE SCANDALOUS STREETS 1-3
FEAR MY GANGSTA 1-5
THESE STREETS DON'T LOVE NOBODY 1-2
BURY ME A G 1-5
A GANGSTA'S EMPIRE 1-4
THE DOPEMAN'S BODYGAURD 1&2
THE REALEST KILLAZ 1-3
THE LAST OF THE OGS 1-3
By **Tranay Adams**

MARRIED TO A BOSS 1-3
By **Destiny Skai & Chris Green**

KINGZ OF THE GAME 1-7
CRIME BOSS 1-4
By **Playa Ray**

FUK SHYT
By **Blakk Diamond**

DON'T F#CK WITH MY HEART 1&2
By **Linnea**

ADDICTED TO THE DRAMA 1-3
IN THE ARM OF HIS BOSS
By **Jamila**

LOYALTY AIN'T PROMISED 1&2
By **Keith Williams**

YAYO 1-4
A SHOOTER'S AMBITION 1&2
BRED IN THE GAME

By **S. Allen**

TRAP GOD 1-3
RICH $AVAGE 1-3
MONEY IN THE GRAVE 1-3
CARTEL MONEY 1&2
By **Martell Troublesome Bolden**

FOREVER GANGSTA 1&2
GLOCKS ON SATIN SHEETS 1&2
By **Adrian Dulan**

TOE TAGZ 1-4
LEVELS TO THIS SHYT 1&2
IT'S JUST ME AND YOU
By **Ah'Million**

KINGPIN DREAMS 1-3
RAN OFF ON DA PLUG
By **Paper Boi Rari**

THE STREETS MADE ME 1-3
By **Larry D. Wright**

CONFESSIONS OF A GANGSTA 1-4
CONFESSIONS OF A JACKBOY 1-3
CONFESSIONS OF A HITMAN
CONFESSIONS OF A DOPE BOY
By **Nicholas Lock**

I'M NOTHING WITHOUT HIS LOVE
SINS OF A THUG
TO THE THUG I LOVED BEFORE
A GANGSTA SAVED XMAS
IN A HUSTLER I TRUST
By **Monet Dragun**

QUIET MONEY 1-3

THUG LIFE 1-3
EXTENDED CLIP 1&2
A GANGSTA'S PARADISE
By **Trai'Quan**

CAUGHT UP IN THE LIFE 1-3
THE STREETS NEVER LET GO 1-3
By **Robert Baptiste**

NEW TO THE GAME 1-3
MONEY, MURDER & MEMORIES 1-3
By **Malik D. Rice**

CREAM 2-3
THE STREETS WILL TALK
By **Yolanda Moore**

THE STREETS WILL NEVER CLOSE 1-3
By **K'ajji**

LIFE OF A SAVAGE 1-4
A GANGSTA'S QUR'AN 1-4
MURDA SEASON 1-3
GANGLAND CARTEL 1-3
CHI'RAQ GANGSTAS 1-4
KILLERS ON ELM STREET 1-3
JACK BOYZ N DA BRONX 1-3
A DOPEBOY'S DREAM 1-3
JACK BOYS VS DOPE BOYS 1-3
COKE GIRLZ
COKE BOYS
SOSA GANG 1&2
BRONX SAVAGES
BODYMORE KINGPINS
BLOOD OF A GOON
By **Romell Tukes**

CONCRETE KILLA 1-3
VICIOUS LOYALTY 1-3

BLOODY MONEY BAGS
By **Kingpen**

THE ULTIMATE SACRIFICE 1-6
KHADIFI
IF YOU CROSS ME ONCE 1-3
ANGEL 1-4
IN THE BLINK OF AN EYE
By **Anthony Fields**

THE LIFE OF A HOOD STAR
By **Ca$h & Rashia Wilson**

NIGHTMARES OF A HUSTLA 1-3
BLOOD AND GAMES 1&2
By **King Dream**

GHOST MOB
By **Stilloan Robinson**

HARD AND RUTHLESS 1&2
MOB TOWN 251
THE BILLIONAIRE BENTLEYS 1-3
REAL G'S MOVE IN SILENCE
By **Von Diesel**

MOB TIES 1-7
SOUL OF A HUSTLER, HEART OF A KILLER 1-3
GORILLAZ IN THE TRENCHES
OOPS CRY TOO 1&2
THE DAUGHTER OF A CARTEL BOSS
By **SayNoMore**

BODYMORE MURDERLAND 1-3
THE BIRTH OF A GANGSTER 1-4
By **Delmont Player**

FOR THE LOVE OF A BOSS 1&2

KILLAZ ON STANDBY 2 | IRA B

By **C. D. Blue**

KILLA KOUNTY 1-5
TENDER
By **Khufu**

MOBBED UP 1-4
THE BRICK MAN 1-5
THE COCAINE PRINCESS 1-10
STEPPERS 1-3
SUPER GREMLIN 1-4
A GANGSTA'S SON
By **King Rio**

MONEY GAME 1&2
By **Smoove Dolla**

A GANGSTA'S KARMA 1-5
By **FLAME**

KING OF THE TRENCHES 1-3
By **GHOST & TRANAY ADAMS**

BAD BITCHES WIT GUNZ 1&2
PROBLEM SOLVED
By **"Christopher Diesel" Hornezes**

QUEEN OF THE ZOO 1&2
By **Black Migo**

GRIMEY WAYS 1-3
BETRAYAL OF A G
By **Ray Vinci**

XMAS WITH AN ATL SHOOTER
By **Ca$h & Destiny Skai**

KING KILLA 1&2
By **Vincent "Vitto" Holloway**

BETRAYAL OF A THUG 1&2
By **Fre$h**

COUNTDOWN OF A KILLA 1&2
SEX, MURDER AND GOD 1&2
GUNS DOWN, BOTTOMS UP 1&2
By Lo-Life

THE MURDER QUEENS 1-7
By **Michael Gallon**

FOR THE LOVE OF BLOOD 1-4
By **Jamel Mitchell**

HOOD CONSIGLIERE 1&2
NO TIME FOR ERROR
By **Keese**

PROTÉGÉ OF A LEGEND 1,2&3
LOVE IN THE TRENCHES 1&2
By **Corey Robinson**

THE PLUG'S RUTHLESS DAUGHTER 1&2
By **Tony Daniels**

BORN IN THE GRAVE 1-3
CRIME PAYS
By **Self Made Tay**

MOAN IN MY MOUTH
By **XTASY**

TORN BETWEEN A GANGSTER AND A GENTLEMAN
By **J-BLUNT & Miss Kim**

LOYALTY IS EVERYTHING 1-3
CITY OF SMOKE 1-3
By **Molotti**

HERE TODAY GONE TOMORROW 1&2
By **Fly Rock**

WOMEN LIE MEN LIE 1-4
FIFTY SHADES OF SNOW 1-3
STACK BEFORE YOU SPLURGE
GIRLS FALL LIKE DOMINOES
NAÏVE TO THE STREETS
By **ROY MILLIGAN**

PILLOW PRINCESS
By **S. Hawkins**

THE BUTTERFLY MAFIA 1-3
SALUTE MY SAVAGERY 1&2
By **Fumiya Payne**

THE LANE 1&2
By Ken-Ken Spence

THE PUSSY TRAP 1-5
By **Nene Capri**

DIRTY DNA
By **Blaque**

SANCTIFIED AND HORNY
by **XTASY**

BOOKS BY LDP'S CEO, CA$II

TRUST IN NO MAN
TRUST IN NO MAN 2
TRUST IN NO MAN 3

BONDED BY BLOOD
SHORTY GOT A THUG
THUGS CRY
THUGS CRY 2
THUGS CRY 3
TRUST NO BITCH
TRUST NO BITCH 2
TRUST NO BITCH 3
TIL MY CASKET DROPS
RESTRAINING ORDER
RESTRAINING ORDER 2
IN LOVE WITH A CONVICT
LIFE OF A HOOD STAR
XMAS WITH AN ATL SHOOTER

***

Other services available upon request.
Additional charges may apply

Lock Down Publications
P.O. Box 944
Stockbridge, GA 30281-9998
Phone: 470 303-9761
Email: lockdownpublications@gmail.com

Submission Guideline

Submit the first three chapters of your completed manuscript to ldpsubmissions@gmail.com. In the subject line add **Your Book's Title**. The manuscript must be in a Word Doc file and sent as an attachment. Document should be in Times New Roman, double spaced, and in size 12 font. Also, provide your synopsis and full contact information. If sending multiple submissions, they must each be in a separate email.

Have a story but no way to send it electronically? You can still submit to LDP/Ca$h Presents. Send in the first three chapters, written or typed, of your completed manuscript to:

LDP: Submissions Dept
P.O. Box 944
Stockbridge, GA 30281-9998

DO NOT send original manuscript. Must be a duplicate. Provide your synopsis and a cover letter containing your full contact information.

Thanks for considering LDP and Ca$h Presents.

www.ingramcontent.com/pod-product-compliance
Lightning Source LLC
Chambersburg PA
CBHW060424260626
47161CB00005B/1773